A Long Day in November

The Dial Press :: New York

Ernest J. Gaines A Long
Day in November

drawings by Don Bolognese

*This book is dedicated to
all those children who have had
One Long Day in their lives.*

A Long Day in November

I

Somebody is shaking me, but I don't want get up now because I'm tired and I'm sleepy and I don't want get up now. It's warm under the cover here, but it's cold up there and I don't want get up now.

"Sonny?" I hear.

But I don't want get up, because it's cold up there. The cover is over my head and I'm under the sheet and the blanket and the quilt. It's warm under here and it's dark, because my eyes's shut. I keep my eyes shut because I don't want get up.

"Sonny?" I hear.

I don't know who's calling me, but it must be Mama because I'm home. I don't know who it is because I'm still asleep, but it must be Mama. She's shaking me by the foot. She's holding my ankle through the cover.

"Wake up, honey," she says.

But I don't want get up because it's cold up there and I don't want get cold. I try to go back to sleep, but she shakes my foot again.

"Hummm?" I say.

"Wake up, honey," I hear.

"Hummm?" I say.

"I want you get up and wee-wee," she says.

"I don't want wee-wee, Mama," I say.

"Come on," she says, shaking me. "Come on. Get up for Mama."

"It's cold up there," I say.

"Come on," she says. "Mama won't let her baby get cold."

I pull the sheet and blanket from under my head and push them back over my shoulder. I feel the cold and I try to cover up again, but Mama grabs the cover before I get it over me. Mama is standing 'side the bed and she's looking down at me, smiling.

The room is dark. The lamp's on the mantelpiece, but it's kind of low. I see Mama's shadow on the wall over by Gran'mon's picture.

"I'm cold, Mama," I say.

"Mama go'n wrap his little coat round her baby," she says.

She goes over and get it off the chair where all my clothes's at, and I sit up in the bed. Mama brings the coat and put it on me, and she fastens some of the buttons.

"Now," she says. "See? You warm."

I gap' and look at Mama. She hugs me real hard and rubs her face against my face. My mama's face is warm and soft, and it feels good.

"I want my socks on," I say. "My feet go'n get cold on the floor."

Mama leans over and get my shoes from under the bed. She takes out my socks and slip them on my feet. I gap' and look at Mama pulling my socks up.

"Now," she says.

I get up, but I can still feel that cold floor. I get on my knees and look under the bed for my pot.

"See it?" Mama says.

"Hanh?"

"See it under there?"

"Hanh?"

"I bet you didn't bring it in," she says. "Any time you sound like that, you done forgot it."

"I left it on the chicken coop," I say.

"Well, go to the back door," Mama says. "Hurry up before you get cold."

I get off my knees and go back there, but it's too dark and I can't see. I come back where Mama's sitting on my bed.

"It's dark back there, Mama," I say. "I might trip over something."

Mama takes a deep breath and gets the lamp off the mantelpiece, and me and her go back in the kitchen. She unlatches the door, and I crack it open and the cold air comes in.

"Hurry," Mama says.

"All right."

I can see the fence back of the house and I can see the little pecan tree over by the toilet. I can see the big pecan tree over by the other fence by Miss Viola Brown's house. Miss Viola Brown must be sleeping because it's late at night. I bet you nobody else in the quarter's up now. I bet you I'm the only little boy up. They got plenty stars in the air, but I can't see the moon. There must be ain't no moon tonight.

That grass is shining—and it must be done rained. That pecan tree's shadow's all over the back yard.

I get my tee-tee and I wee-wee. I wee-wee hard, because I don't want get cold. Mama latches the door when I get through wee-wee-ing.

"I want some water, Mama," I say.

"Let it out and put it right back in, huh?" Mama says.

She dips up some water and pours it in my cup, and I drink. I don't drink too much at once, because the water makes my teeth cold. I let my teeth warm up, and I drink some more.

"I got enough," I say.

Mama drinks the rest and then me and her go back in the front room.

"Sonny?" she says.

"Hanh?"

"Tomorrow morning when you get up, me and you leaving here, hear?"

"Where we going?" I ask.

"We going to Gran'mom," Mama says.

"We leaving us house?" I ask.

"Yes," she says.

"Daddy leaving too?"

"No," she says. "Just me and you."

"Daddy don't want leave?"

"I don't know what your daddy wants," Mama says. "But for sure he don't want me. We leaving, hear?"

"Uh-huh," I say.

"I'm tired of it," Mama says.

"Hanh?"

"You won't understand, honey," Mama says. "You too young still."

"I'm getting cold, Mama," I say.

"All right," she says. She goes and put the lamp up, and comes back and sit on the bed 'side me. "Let me take your socks off," she says.

"I can take them off," I say.

Mama takes my coat off and I take my socks off. I get back in bed and Mama pulls the cover up over me. She leans over and kiss me on the jaw, and then she goes back to her bed. Mama's bed is over by the window. My bed is by the fireplace. I hear Mama get in the bed. I hear the spring, then I don't hear nothing because Mama's quiet. Then I hear Mama crying.

"Mama?" I call.

She don't answer me.

"Mama?" I call her.

"Go to sleep, baby," she says.

"You crying?" I ask.

"Go to sleep," Mama says.

"I don't want you to cry," I say.

"Mama's not crying," she says.

Then I don't hear nothing and I lay quiet, but I don't turn over because my spring'll make noise and I don't want make no noise because I want hear if my mama go'n cry again. I don't hear Mama no more and I feel warm in the bed, and I pull the cover over my head and I feel good. I don't hear nothing no more and I feel myself going back to sleep.

Billy Joe Martin's got the tire and he's rolling it in the road, and I run to the gate to look at him. I want go out in the road, but Mama don't want me to play out there like Billy Joe Martin and the other children. . . . Lucy's playing 'side the house. She's jumping rope with—I don't know who that is. I go 'side the house and play with Lucy. Lucy beats me jumping rope. The rope keeps on hitting me on the leg. But it don't hit Lucy on the leg. Lucy jumps too high for it. . . . Me and Billy Joe Martin shoots marbles and I beat him shooting. . . . Mama's sweeping the gallery and knocking the dust out of the broom on the side of the house. Mama keeps on knocking the broom against the wall. Must be got plenty dust in the broom.

Somebody's beating on the door. Mama, some-body's beating on the door. Somebody's beating on the door, Mama.

"Amy, please let me in," I hear.

Somebody's beating on the door, Mama. Mama, somebody's beating on the door.

"Amy, honey; honey, please let me in."

I push the cover back and I listen. I hear Daddy beating on the door.

"Mama?" I say. "Mama, Daddy's knocking on the door. He want come in."

"Go back to sleep, Sonny," Mama says.

"Daddy's out there," I say. "He want come in."

"Go back to sleep, I told you," Mama says.

I lay back on my pillow and listen.

"Amy," Daddy says, "I know you woke. Open the door."

Mama don't answer him.

"Amy, honey," Daddy says. "My sweet dumpling, let me in. It's freezing out here."

Mama still won't answer Daddy.

"Mama?" I say.

"Go back to sleep, Sonny," she says.

"Mama, Daddy want come in," I say.

"Let him crawl through the key hole," Mama says.

It gets quiet after this, and it stays quiet a little while, and then Daddy says, "Sonny?"

"Hanh?"

"Come open the door for your daddy."

"Mama go'n whip me if I get up," I say.

"I won't let her whip you," Daddy says. "Come and open the door like a good boy."

I push the cover back and I sit up in the bed and look over at Mama's bed. Mama's under the cover and she's quiet like she's asleep. I get on the floor and get my socks out of my shoes. I get back in the bed and slip them on, and then I go and unlatch the door for Daddy. Daddy comes in and rubs my head with his hand. His hand is hard and cold.

"Look what I brought you and your mama," he says.

"What?" I ask.

Daddy takes a paper bag out of his jumper pocket.

"Candy?" I say.

"Uh-huh."

Daddy opens the bag and I stick my hand in there and take a whole handful. Daddy wraps the bag up

again and sticks it in his pocket.

"Get back in that bed, Sonny," Mama says.

"I'm eating candy," I say.

"Get back in that bed like I told you," Mama says.

"Daddy's up with me," I say.

"You heard me, boy?"

"You can take your candy with you," Daddy says. "Get back in the bed."

He follows me to the bed and tucks the cover under me. I lay in the bed and eat my candy. The candy is hard, and I sound just like Paul eating corn. I bet you little old Paul is some cold out there in that back yard. I hope he ain't laying in that water like he always do. I bet you he'll freeze in that water in all this cold. I'm sure glad I ain't a pig. They ain't got no mama and no daddy and no house.

I hear the spring when Daddy gets in the bed.

"Honey?" Daddy says.

Mama don't answer him.

"Honey?" he says.

Mama must be gone back to sleep, because she don't answer him.

"Honey?" Daddy says.

"Don't touch me," Mama says.

"Honey," Daddy says. Then he starts crying. "Honey, I'm sorry. I'm sorry."

Daddy cries a good little while, and then he stops. I don't chew on my candy while Daddy's crying, but when he stops, I chew on another piece.

"Go to sleep, Sonny," he says.

"I want eat my candy," I say.

"Hurry then. You got to go to school tomorrow."

I put another piece in my mouth and chew on it.

"Honey?" I hear Daddy saying. "Honey, you go'n wake me up to go to work?"

"I do hope you stop bothering me," Mama says.

"Wake me up round four thirty, hear, honey?" Daddy says. "I can cut 'bout six tons tomorrow. Maybe seven."

Mama don't say nothing to Daddy, and I feel sleepy again. I finish chewing my last piece of candy and I turn on my side. I feel good because the bed is warm. But I still got my socks on.

"Daddy?" I call.

"Go to sleep," Daddy says.

"My socks still on," I say.

"Let them stay on tonight," Daddy says. "Go to sleep."

"My feet don't feel good in socks," I say.

"Please go to sleep, Sonny," Daddy says. "I got to get up at four thirty, and it's hitting close to two now."

I don't say nothing, but I don't like to sleep with my socks on. But I stay quiet. Daddy and Mama don't say nothing, either, and little bit later I hear Daddy snoring. I feel drowsy myself.

I run around the house in the mud because it done rained, and I feel the mud between my toes. The mud is soft and I like to play in it. I try to get out the mud, but I can't get out. I'm not stuck in the mud, but I can't get out. Lucy can't come over and play in the mud because her mama don't want her to catch cold. . . . Billy Joe Martin shows me his dime and puts it back in his pocket. Mama bought me a pretty little red coat and I show it to Lucy. But I don't let Billy Joe Martin put his hand on it. Lucy can touch it all she wants, but I don't let Billy Joe Martin put his hand on it. . . . Me and Lucy get on the horse and ride up and down the road. The horse runs fast, and me and Lucy bounce on the horse and laugh. . . . Mama and Daddy and Uncle Al and Gran'mon's sitting by the fire talking. I'm outside shooting marbles, but I hear them. I don't know what they talking about, but I hear them. I hear them. I hear them. I hear them.

I don't want wake up, but I'm waking up. Mama and Daddy's talking. I want go back to sleep, but they talking too loud. I feel my foot in the sock. I don't like socks on when I'm in the bed. I want go back to sleep, but I can't. Mama and Daddy talking too much.

"Honey, you let me oversleep," Daddy says. "Look here, it's going on seven o'clock."

"You ought to been thought about that last night." Mama says.

"Honey, please," Daddy says. "Don't start a fuss right off this morning."

"Then don't open your mouth," Mama says.

"Honey, the car broke down," Daddy says. "What I was suppose to do, it broke down on me. I just couldn't walk away and not try to fix it."

Mama's quiet.

"Honey," Daddy says, "don't be mad with me. Come, give your man a good little kiss so he can get out of here."

"Go kiss your car," Mama says.

"Kiss my car?" Daddy says. "That cold car? Honey, you don't mean that."

"I mean just that," she says.

"Honey, I been kissing you every morning since us been married," Daddy says. "I kiss you and you kiss me—and that's how I been making it in that world out there. How I'm go'n stop it now?"

"That's up to you," Mama says.

"Honey," Daddy says. "This is Eddie your husband. The one you married. Remember?"

"You married to that car," Mama says. "Go kiss her. I'm sure she waiting. I ain't."

"Honey," Daddy says, "suppose Sonny hear you talking like that? Didn't that preacher say we had to set a good sample for him?"

"Then how come you don't set a good sample for him?" Mama says. "How come you don't come home sometime and set a good sample for him? How come you can't leave that car alone long enough to set a good sample for him? You the one need to set a good sample. You the one. I do my best."

"Honey, I told you before the car broke down on me," Daddy says. "I was coming home when it broke down. I even had to leave it out on the road. I made it here quick as I could."

"You can go back quick as you can, for all I care," Mama says.

"Honey, you don't mean that," Daddy says. "I

know you don't mean that. You just saying that because you mad."

"Just don't touch me," Mama says.

"Honey, I got to get out and make some bread for us," Daddy says.

"Get out if you want," Mama says. "They got a jailhouse for them who don't support their family."

"Honey, please don't talk about a jail," Daddy says. "It's too cold. You don't know how cold it is in a jailhouse this time of the year."

Mama's quiet.

"Honey?" Daddy says.

"I hope you let me go back to sleep," Mama says. "Please."

"Honey, don't go back to sleep on me," Daddy says. "Honey—"

"I'm getting up," Mama says. "Damn all this."

I hear the springs mash down on the bed boards. My head's under the cover, but I can just see Mama pushing the cover down the bed. Then I hear her walking across the floor and going back in the kitchen.

"Oh, Lord," Daddy says. "Oh, Lord. The suffering a man got to go through in this world. Sonny?" he says.

"Don't wake that baby up," Mama says, from the door.

"I got to have somebody to talk to," Daddy says. "Sonny?"

"I told you not to wake him up," Mama says.

"You don't want talk to me," Daddy says. "I need somebody to talk to. Sonny?" he says.

"Hanh?"

"See what you did?" Mama says. "You woke him up, and he ain't going back to sleep."

Daddy comes across the floor and sits down on the side of the bed. He looks down at me and passes his hand over my face.

"You love your daddy, Sonny?" he says.

"Uh-huh."

"Please love me," Daddy says.

I look up at Daddy and he looks at me, and then he just falls down on me and starts crying.

"A man needs somebody to love him," he says.

"Get love from what you give love," Mama says, back in the kitchen. "You love your car. Go let it love you back."

Daddy shakes his face in the cover.

"The suffering a man got to go through in this world," he says. "Sonny, I hope you never have to go through all this."

Daddy lays there 'side me a long time. I can hear Mama back in the kitchen. I hear her putting some wood in the stove, and then I hear her lighting the fire. I hear her pouring water in the tea kettle, and I hear when she sets the kettle on the stove.

Daddy raises up and wipes his eyes. He looks at me and shakes his head, then he goes and puts his overalls on.

"It's a hard life," he says. "Hard, hard. One day, Sonny—you too young right now—but one day you'll know what I mean."

"Can I get up, Daddy?"

"Better ask your mama," Daddy says.

"Can I get up, Mama?" I call.

Mama don't answer me.

"Mama?" I call.

"Your pa standing in there," Mama says. "He the one woke you up."

"Can I get up, Daddy?"

"Sonny, I got enough troubles right now," Daddy say.

"I want get up and wee-wee," I say.

"Get up," Mama says. "You go'n worry me till I let you get up anyhow."

I crawl from under the cover and look at my feet. I got just one sock on and I look for the other one under the cover. I find it and slip it on and then I get on the floor. But that floor is still cold. I hurry up and put on my clothes, and I get my shoes and go and sit on the bed to put them on.

Daddy waits till I finish tying up my shoes, and me and him go back in the kitchen. I get in the corner 'side the stove, and Daddy comes over and stands 'side me. The fire is warm and it feels good.

Mama is frying salt meat in the skillet. The skillet's over one hole and the tea kettle's over the other one. The water's boiling, and the tea kettle is whistling. I look at the steam shooting up to the loft.

Mama goes outside and gets my pot. She holds my pot for me and I wee-wee in it. She dumps the wee-wee out the back door and takes my pot to the front.

Daddy pours some water in the wash basin and washes his face, then he washes my face. I shut my eyes tight. I feel Daddy rubbing at my eyes to get them clean. I keep my eyes shut tight so no soap can get in. Daddy opens the back door and pitches the water out on the ground. We go to the table and sit down, and Mama brings the food. She stands there till I get through saying my blessing, then she goes back to the stove and warm. Me and Daddy eat.

"You love your daddy?" he says.

"Uh-huh," I say.

"That's a good boy," he says. "Always love your daddy."

"I love Mama, too. I love her more than I love you."

"You got a good mama," Daddy says. "I love her, too. She the only thing keep me going—'cluding you, too."

I look at Mama standing 'side the stove, warming.

"Why don't you come to the table and eat with us?" Daddy says.

"I'm not hungry," Mama says.

"I'm sorry, baby," Daddy says. "I mean it."

Mama just looks down at the stove and don't answer Daddy.

"You got a right to be mad," Daddy says. "I ain't nothing but a' old rotten dog."

Daddy eats his food and looks at me across the table. I pick up a piece of meat and chew on it. I like the skin because the skin is hard. I keep the skin a long time.

"Well, I better get going," Daddy says. "Maybe if I work hard, I'll get me a couple tons."

Daddy gets up from the table and goes in the front room. He comes back with his jumper and his hat on. Daddy's hat is gray and it got a hole on the side.

"I'm leaving, honey," he tells Mama.

Mama don't answer Daddy.

"Honey, tell me ' 'Bye, old dog,' or something," Daddy says. "Just don't stand there."

Mama still don't answer him, and Daddy jerks his cane knife out the wall and goes on out. I chew on my meat skin. I like it because it's hard.

"Hurry up, honey," Mama says. "We going to Gran'mon."

Mama goes in the front room and I stay at the table and eat. I finish eating and I go in the front room where Mama is. Mama's pulling a big bundle of clothes from under the bed.

"What's that, Mama?" I ask.

"Us clothes," she says.

"We go'n take us clothes down to Gran'mon?"

"I'm go'n try," Mama says. "Find your cap and put it on."

I see my cap hanging on the chair and I put it on and fasten the strap under my chin. Mama fixes my shirt in my pants, and then she goes and puts on her overcoat. Her overcoat is black and her hat is black.

She puts on her hat and looks in the looking glass. I can see her face in the glass. Look like she want cry. She comes from the dresser and looks at the big bundle of clothes on the floor.

"Find your pot," she says.

I get my pot from under the bed.

"Come on," Mama says.

She drags the big bundle of clothes out on the

gallery and I shut the door. Mama squats down and puts the bundle on her head, and then she stands up and me and her go down the steps. Soon's I get out in the road I can feel the wind. It's strong and it's blowing in my face. My face is cold and one of my hands is cold.

It's red over there back of the trees. Mr. Guerin's house is over there. I see Mr. Guerin's big old dog.

He must be don't see me and Mama because he ain't barking at us.

"Don't linger back too far," Mama says.

I run and catch up with Mama. Me and Mama's the only two people walking in the road now.

I look up and I see the tree in Gran'mon's yard. We go little farther and I see the house. I run up ahead of Mama and hold the gate open for her. After she goes in, I let the gate slam.

Spot starts barking soon's he sees me. He runs down the steps at me and I let him smell my pot. Spot follows me and Mama back to the house.

"Gran'mon?" I call.

"Who that out there?" Gran'mon asks.

"Me," I say.

"What you doing out there in all that cold for, boy?" Gran'mon says. I hear Gran'mon coming to the door fussing. She opens the door and looks at me and Mama.

"What you doing here with all that?" she asks.

"I'm leaving him, Mama," Mama says.

"Eddie?" Gran'mon says. "What he done you now?"

"I'm just tired of it," Mama says.

"Come in here out that cold," Gran'mon says.

"Walking out there in all that weather . . ."

We go inside and Mama drops the big bundle of clothes on the floor. I go to the fire and warm my hands. Mama and Gran'mon come to the fire and Mama stands at the other end of the fireplace and warms her hands.

"Now what that no good nigger done done?" Gran'mon asks.

"Mama, I'm just tired of Eddie running up and down the road in that car," Mama says.

"He beat you?" Gran'mon asks.

"No, he didn't beat me," Mama says. "Mama, Eddie didn't get home till after two this morning. Messing around with that old car somewhere out on the road all night."

"I told you," Gran'mon says. "I told you when that nigger got that car that was go'n happen. I told you. No—you wouldn't listen. I told you. Put a fool in a car and he becomes a bigger fool. Where that yellow thing at now?"

"God telling," Mama says. "He left with his cane knife."

"I warned you 'bout that nigger," Gran'mon says. "Even 'fore you married him. I sung at you and sung at you. I said, 'Amy, that nigger ain't no good. A yellow nigger with a gap like that 'tween his front teeth ain't no good.' But you wouldn't listen."

"Can me and Sonny stay here?" Mama asks.

"Where else can y'all go?" Gran'mon says. "I'm your mon, ain't I? You think I can put you out in the cold like he did?"

"He didn't put me out, Mama, I left," Mama says.

"You finally getting some sense in your head," Gran'mon says. "You ought to been left that nigger years ago."

Uncle Al comes in the front room and looks at the bundle of clothes on the floor. Uncle Al's got on his overalls and got just one strap hooked. The other strap's hanging down his back.

"Fix that thing on you," Gran'mon says. "You not in a stable."

Uncle Al fixes his clothes and looks at me and Mama at the fire.

"Y'all had a round?" he asks Mama.

"Eddie and that car again," Mama says.

"That's all they want these days," Gran'mon says. "Cars. Why don't they marry them cars? No. When they got their troubles, they come running to the womenfolks. When they ain't got no troubles and when their pockets full of money, they run jump in the car. I told you that when you was working to help him get that car."

Uncle Al stands 'side me at the fireplace, and I lean against him and look at the steam coming out a piece of wood. Lord knows I get tired of Gran'mon fussing all the time.

"Y'all moving in with us?" Uncle Al asks.

"For a few days," Mama says. "Then I'll try to find another place somewhere in the quarter."

"We got plenty room here," Uncle Al says. "This old man here can sleep with me."

Uncle Al gets a little stick out of the corner and hands it to me so I can light it for him. I hold it to the fire till it's lit, and I hand it back to Uncle Al. Uncle Al turns the pipe upside down in his mouth and holds the fire to it. When the pipe's good and lit, Uncle Al gives me the little stick and I throw it back in the fire.

"Y'all ate anything?" Gran'mon asks.

"Sonny ate," Mama says. "I'm not hungry."

"I reckon you go'n start looking for work now?" Gran'mon says.

"There's plenty cane to cut," Mama says. "I'll get me a cane knife and go out tomorrow morning."

"Out in all that cold?" Gran'mon says.

"They got plenty women cutting cane," Mama says. "I don't mind. I done it before."

"You used to be such a pretty little thing, Amy," Gran'mon says. "Long silky curls. Prettiest little face on this whole plantation. You could've married somebody worth something. But, no, you had to go throw yourself away to that yellow nigger who don't care for nobody, 'cluding himself."

"I loved Eddie," Mama says.

"Poot," Gran'mon says.

"He wasn't like this when we married," Mama says.

"Every nigger from Bayonne like this now, then, and forever," Gran'mon says.

"Not then," Mama says. "He was the sweetest person—"

"And you fell for him?" Gran'mon says.

"He changed after he got that car," Mama says. "He changed overnight."

"Well, you learned your lesson," Gran'mon says. "We all get teached something no matter how old we get. 'Live and learn,' what they say."

"Eddie's all right," Uncle Al says. "He—"

"You keep out of this, Albert," Gran'mon says. "It don't concern you."

Uncle Al don't say no more, and I can feel his hand on my shoulder. I like Uncle Al because he's good, and he never talk bad about Daddy. But Gran'-mon's always talking bad about Daddy.

"Freddie's still there," Gran'mon says.

"Mama, please," Mama says.

"Why not?" Gran'mon says. "He always loved you."

"Not in front of him," Mama says.

Mama leaves the fireplace and goes to the bundle of clothes. I can hear her untying the bundle.

"Ain't it 'bout time you was leaving for school?" Uncle Al asks.

"I don't want go," I say. "It's too cold."

"It's never too cold for school," Mama says. "Warm up good and let Uncle Al button your coat for you."

I get closer to the fire and I feel the fire hot on my pants. I turn around and warm my back. I turn again, and Uncle Al leans over and buttons my coat. Uncle Al's pipe almost gets in my face, and it don't smell good.

"Now," Uncle Al says. "You all ready to go. You want take a potato with you?"

"Uh-huh."

Uncle Al leans over and gets me a potato out of

the ashes. He knocks all the ashes off and puts the potato in my pocket.

"Wait," Mama says. "Mama, don't you have a little paper bag?"

Gran'mon looks on the mantelpiece and gets a paper bag. There's something in the bag, and she takes it out and hands the bag to Mama. Mama puts the potato in the bag and puts it in my pocket. Then she goes and gets my book and tucks it under my arm.

"Now you ready," she says. "And remember, when you get out for dinner, come back here. Don't you forget and go up home now. You hear, Sonny?"

"Uh-huh."

"Come on," Uncle Al says. "I'll open the gate for you."

" 'Bye, Mama," I say.

"Be a good boy," Mama says. "Eat your potato at recess. Don't eat it in class now."

Me and Uncle Al go out on the gallery. The sun is shining but it's still cold out there. Spot follows me and Uncle Al down the walk. Uncle Al opens the gate for me and I go out in the road, I hate to leave Uncle Al and Spot. And I hate to leave Mama—and I hate to leave the fire. But I got to, because they want me to learn.

"See you at twelve," Uncle Al says.

I go up the quarter and Uncle Al and Spot go back to the house. I see all the children going to school. But I don't see Lucy. When I get to her house, I'm go'n stop at the gate and call her. She must be don't want go to school, cold as it is.

It still got some ice in the water. I better not walk in the water. I'll get my feet wet, and Mama'll whip me.

When I get closer, I look and I see Lucy and her mama on the gallery. Lucy's mama ties her bonnet for her, and Lucy comes down the steps. She runs down the walk toward the gate. Lucy's bonnet is red and her coat is red.

"Hi," I say.

"Hi," she says.

"It's some cold," I say.

"Unnn-hunnnn," Lucy says.

Me and Lucy walk side by side up the quarter. Lucy's got her book in her book sack.

"We moved," I say. "We staying with Gran'mon now."

"Y'all moved?" Lucy asks.

"Uh-huh."

"Y'all didn't move," Lucy says. "When y'all moved?"

"This morning."

"Who moved y'all?" Lucy asks.

"Me and Mama," I say. "I'm go'n sleep with Uncle Al."

"My legs getting cold," Lucy says.

"I got a potato," I say. "In my pocket."

"You go'n eat it and give me piece?" Lucy says.

"Uh-huh." I say. "At recess."

Me and Lucy walk up the quarter, and Lucy stops and touches the ice with her shoe.

"You go'n get your foot wet," I say.

"No, I'm not," Lucy says.

Lucy breaks the ice with her shoe and laughs. I laugh and I break a piece of ice with my shoe. Me and Lucy laugh and I see the smoke coming out of Lucy's mouth. I open my mouth and go "Haaaa" and plenty smoke comes out of my mouth. Lucy laughs and points at the smoke.

Me and Lucy go on up the quarter to the schoolhouse. Billy Joe Martin and Ju-Ju and them's playing marbles right by the gate. Over 'side the schoolhouse Shirley and Dottie and Katie's jumping rope. On the other side of the schoolhouse some more children playing "Patty-cake, patty-cake, baker-man" to keep warm. Lucy goes where Shirley and them's jumping rope and asks them to play. I stop where Billy Joe Martin and them's at and watch them shoot marbles.

II

It's warm inside the schoolhouse. Bill made a big
fire in the heater, and I can hear it roaring up the
pipes. I look out the window and I can see the smoke
flying across the yard. Bill sure knows how to make a
good fire. Bill's the biggest boy in school, and he
always makes the fire for us.

Everybody's studying their lesson, but I don't
know mine. I wish I knowed it, but I don't. Mama
didn't teach me my lesson last night, and she didn't
teach it to me this morning, and I don't know it.

"Bob and Rex in the yard. Rex is barking at the cow." I don't know what all this other reading is. I see "Rex" again, and I see "cow" again—but I don't know what all the rest of it is.

Bill comes up to the heater and I look up and see him putting another piece of wood in the fire. He goes back to his seat and sits down 'side Juanita. Miss Hebert looks at Bill when he goes back to his seat. I look in my book at Bob and Rex. Bob's got on a white shirt and blue pants. Rex is a German police dog. He's white and brown. Mr. Bouie's got a dog just like Rex. He don't bite though. He's a good dog. But Mr. Guerin's old dog'll bite you for sure. I seen him this morning when me and Mama was going down to Gran'mon's house.

I ain't go'n eat dinner at us house because me and Mama don't stay there no more. I'm go'n eat at Gran'mon's house. I don't know where Daddy go'n eat dinner. He must be go'n cook his own dinner.

I can hear Bill and Juanita back of me. They whispering to each other, but I can hear them. Juanita's some pretty. I wish I was big so I could love her. But I better look at my lesson and don't think about other things.

"First grade," Miss Hebert says.

We go up to the front and sit down on the bench. Miss Hebert looks at us and make a mark in her roll book. She puts the roll book down and comes over to the bench where we at.

"Does everyone know his lesson today?" she asks.

"Yes ma'am," Lucy says, louder than anybody else in the whole schoolhouse.

"Good," Miss Hebert says. "And I'll start with you today, Lucy. Hold your book in one hand and begin."

" 'Bob and Rex are in the yard,' " Lucy reads. " 'Rex is barking at the cow. The cow is watching Rex.' "

"Good," Miss Hebert says. "Point to barking."

Lucy points.

"Good, now point to watching."

Lucy points again.

"Good," Miss Hebert says. "Shirley Ann, let's see how well you can read."

I look in the book at Bob and Rex. "Rex is barking at the cow. The cow is looking at Rex."

"William Joseph," Miss Hebert says.

I'm next, I'm scared. I don't know my lesson and Miss Hebert go'n whip me. Miss Hebert don't like you when you don't know your lesson. I can see her strap over there on the table. I can see the clock and the little bell, too. Bill split the end of the strap, and them little ends sting some. Soon's Billy Joe Martin finishes, then it's me. I don't know . . . Mama ought to been . . . "Bob and Rex" . . .

"Eddie," Miss Hebert says.

I don't know my lesson. I don't know my lesson. I don't know my lesson. I feel warm. I'm wet. I hear the wee-wee dripping on the floor. I'm crying. I'm crying because I wee-wee on myself. My clothes's wet. Lucy and them go'n laugh at me. Billy Joe Mar-

tin and them go'n tease me. I don't know my lesson. I don't know my lesson. I don't know my lesson.

"Oh, Eddie, look what you've done," I think I hear Miss Hebert saying. I don't know if she's saying this, but I think I hear her say it. My eyes's shut and I'm crying. I don't want look at none of them, because I know they laughing at me.

"It's running under that bench there now," Billy Joe Martin says. "Look out for your feet back there, it's moving fast."

"William Joseph," Miss Hebert says. "Go over there and stand in that corner. Turn your face to the wall and stay there until I tell you to move."

I hear Billy Joe Martin leaving the bench, and then it's quiet. But I don't open my eyes.

"Eddie," Miss Hebert says, "go stand by the heater."

I don't move because I'll see them, and I don't want see them.

"Eddie?" Miss Hebert says.

But I don't answer her, and I don't move.

"Bill?" Miss Hebert says.

I hear Bill coming up to the front and then I feel him taking me by the hand and leading me away. I walk with my eyes shut. Me and Bill stop at the heater, because I can feel the fire. Then Bill takes my book and leaves me standing there.

"Juanita," Miss Hebert says, "get a mop, will you please."

I hear Juanita going to the back, and then I hear her coming back to the front. The fire pops in the heater, but I don't open my eyes. Nobody's saying anything, but I know they all watching me.

When Juanita gets through mopping up the wee-wee, she carries the mop back to the closet, and I hear Miss Hebert going on with the lesson. When she gets through with the first graders, she calls the second graders up there.

Bill comes up to the heater and puts another piece of wood in the fire.

"Want turn around?" he asks me.

I don't answer him, but I got my eyes open now, and I'm looking down at the floor. Bill turns me round so I can dry the back of my pants. He pats me on the shoulder and goes back to his seat.

After Miss Hebert gets through with the second graders, she tells the children they can go out for recess. I can hear them getting their coats and hats. When they all leave, I raise my head. I still see Bill and Juanita and Veta sitting there. Bill smiles at me, but I don't smile back. My clothes's dry now, and I feel better. I know the rest of the children go'n tease me, though.

"Bill, why don't you and the rest of the seventh graders put your arithmetic problems on the board," Miss Hebert says. "We'll look at them after recess."

Bill and them stand up, and I watch them go to the blackboard in the back.

"Eddie?" Miss Hebert says.

I turn and I see her sitting behind her desk. And I see Billy Joe Martin standing in the corner with his face to the wall.

"Come up to the front," Miss Hebert says.

I go up there looking down at the floor, because I know she go'n whip me now.

"William Joseph, you may leave," Miss Hebert says.

Billy Joe Martin runs over and gets his coat, and then he runs outside to shoot marbles. I stand in front of Miss Hebert's desk with my head down.

"Look up," she says.

I raise my head and look at Miss Hebert. She's smiling, and she don't look mad.

"Now," she says. "Did you study your lesson last night?"

"Yes, ma'am," I say.

"I want the truth now," she says. "Did you?"

It's a sin to story in the churchhouse, but I'm scared Miss Hebert go'n whip me.

"Yes, ma'am," I say.

"Did you study it this morning?" she asks.

"Yes, ma'am," I say.

"Then why didn't you know it?" she asks.

I feel a big knot coming up in my throat and I feel like I'm go'n cry again. I'm scared Miss Hebert go'n whip me, that's why I story to her.

"You didn't study your lesson, did you?" she says.

I shake my head. "No, ma'am."

"You didn't study it last night either, did you?"

"No, ma'am," I say. "Mama didn't have time to help me. Daddy wasn't home. Mama didn't have time to help me."

"Where is your father?" Miss Hebert asks.

"Cutting cane."

"Here on this place?"

"Yes, ma'am," I say.

Miss Hebert looks at me, and then she gets out a pencil and starts writing on a piece of paper. I look at her writing and I look at the clock and the strap. I can hear the clock. I can hear Billy Joe Martin and them shooting marbles outside. I can hear Lucy and them jumping rope, and some more children playing "Patty-cake."

"I want you to give this to your mother or your father when you get home," Miss Hebert says. "This is only a little note saying I would like to see them sometime when they aren't too busy."

"We don't live home no more," I say.

"Oh?" Miss Hebert says. "Did you move?"

"Me and Mama," I say. "But Daddy didn't."

Miss Hebert looks at me, and then she writes some more on the note. She puts her pencil down and folds the note up.

"Be sure to give this to your mother," she says. "Put it in your pocket and don't lose it."

I take the note from Miss Hebert, but I don't leave the desk.

"Do you want to go outside?" she asks.

"Yes, ma'am."

"You may leave," she says.

I go over and get my coat and cap, and then I go out in the yard. I see Billy Joe Martin and Charles and them shooting marbles over by the gate. I don't go over there because they'll tease me. I go 'side the schoolhouse and look at Lucy and them jumping rope. Lucy ain't jumping right now.

"Hi, Lucy," I say.

Lucy looks over at Shirley and they laugh. They look at my pants and laugh.

"You want a piece of potato?" I ask Lucy.

"No," Lucy says. "And you not my boyfriend no more, either."

I look at Lucy and I go stand 'side the wall in the sun. I peel my potato and eat it. And look like soon 's I get through, Miss Hebert comes to the front and says recess is over.

We go back inside, and I go to the back and take off my coat and cap. Bill comes back there and hang the things up for us. I go over to Miss Hebert's desk and Miss Hebert gives me my book. I go back to my seat and sit down 'side Lucy.

"Hi, Lucy," I say.

Lucy looks at Shirley and Shirley puts her hand over her mouth and laughs. I feel like getting up from there and socking Shirley in the mouth, but I know Miss Hebert'll whip me because I got no business socking people after I done wee-wee on myself. I open my book and look at my lesson so I don't have to look at none of them.

III

It's almost dinner time, and when I get home, I ain't coming back here either, now. I'm go'n stay there. I'm go'n stay right there and sit by the fire. Lucy and them don't want play with me, and I ain't coming back up here. Miss Hebert go'n touch that little bell in a little while. She getting ready to touch it right now.

Soon 's Miss Hebert touches the bell, all the children run go get their hats and coats. I unhook my coat and drop it on the bench till I put my cap on.

Then I put my coat on, and I get my book and leave.

I see Bill and Juanita going out the schoolyard, and I run and catch up with them. Time I get there, I hear Billy Joe Martin and them coming up behind us.

"Look at that baby," Billy Joe Martin says.

"Piss on himself," Ju-Ju says.

"Y'all leave him alone," Bill says.

"Baby, baby, piss on himself," Billy Joe Martin sings.

"What did I say now?" Bill says.

"Piss on himself," Billy Joe Martin says.

"Wait," Bill says. "Let me take off my belt."

"Good-bye, piss pot," Billy Joe Martin says. Him and Ju-Ju run down the road. They spank their hind parts with their hands and run like horses.

"They just bad," Juanita says.

"Don't pay them no mind," Bill says. "They'll leave you alone."

We go on down the quarter and Bill and Juanita hold hands. I go to Gran'mon's gate and open it. I look at Bill and Juanita going down the quarter. They walking close together, and Juanita done put her head on Bill's shoulder. I like to see Bill and

Juanita like that. It makes me feel good. But I go in the yard and I don't feel good any more. I know old Gran'mon go'n start her fussing. Lord in Heaven knows I get tired of all this fussing, day and night. Spot runs down the walk to meet me. I put my hand on his head and me and him go back to the gallery. I make him stay on the gallery, because Gran'mon don't want him inside. I pull the door open and I see Gran'mon and Uncle Al sitting by the fire. I look for my mama, but I don't see her.

"Where Mama?" I ask Uncle Al.

"In the kitchen," Gran'mon says. "But she talking to somebody."

I go back to the kitchen.

"Come back here," Gran'mon says.

"I want see my mama," I say.

"You'll see her when she come out," Gran'mon says.

"I want see my mama now," I say.

"Don't you hear me talking to you, boy?" Gran'mon hollers.

"What's the matter?" Mama asks. Mama comes out of the kitchen and Mr. Freddie Jackson comes out of there, too. I hate Mr. Freddie Jackson. I never did like him. He always want to be round my mama.

"That boy don't listen to nobody," Gran'mon says.

"Hi, Sonny," Mr. Freddie Jackson says.

I look at him standing there, but I don't speak to him. I take the note out of my pocket and hand it to my mama.

"What's this?" Mama says.

"Miss Hebert sent it."

Mama unfolds the note and take it to the fireplace to read it. I can see her mouth working. When she gets through reading, she folds the note up again.

"She want see me or Eddie sometime when we free," Mama says. "Sonny been doing pretty bad in his class."

"I can just see that nigger husband of yours in a schoolhouse," Gran'mon says. "I doubt if he ever went to one."

"Mama, please," Mama says.

Mama helps me off with my coat and I go to the fireplace and stand 'side Uncle Al. Uncle Al pulls me between his legs and he holds my hand out to the fire.

"Well?" I hear Gran'mon saying.

"You know how I feel 'bout her," Mr. Freddie Jackson says. "My house opened to her and Sonny any time she want come there."

"Well?" Gran'mon says.

"Mama, I'm still married to Eddie," Mama says.

"You mean you still love that yellow thing," Gran'mon says. "That's what you mean, ain't it?"

"I didn't say that," Mama says. "What would people say, out one house and in another one the same day?"

"Who care what people say?" Gran'mon says. "Let people say what they big enough to say. You looking out for yourself, not what people say."

"You understand, don't you, Freddie?" Mama says.

"I think I do," he says. "But like I say, Amy, any time—you know that."

"And there ain't no time like right now," Gran'mon says. "You can take that bundle of clothes down there for her."

"Let her make up her own mind, Rachel," Uncle Al says. "She can make up her own mind."

"If you know what's good for you you better keep out of this," Gran'mon says. "She my daughter and if she ain't got sense enough to look out for herself, I have. What you want to do, go out in that field cutting cane in the morning?"

"I don't mind it," Mama says.

"You done forgot how hard cutting cane is?" Gran'mon says. "You must be done forgot."

"I ain't forgot," Mama says. "But if the other women can do it, I suppose I can do it, too."

"Now you talking back," Gran'mon says.

"I'm not talking back, Mama," Mama says. "I just feel it ain't right to leave one house and go to another house the same day. That ain't right in nobody's book."

"Maybe she's right, Mrs. Rachel," Mr. Freddie Jackson says.

"Trouble with her, she still in love with that yellow thing," Gran'mon says. "That's your trouble. You ain't satisfied 'less he got you doing all the work while he rip and run up and down the road with his other nigger friends. No, you ain't satisfied."

Gran'mon goes back in the kitchen fussing. After she leaves the fire, everything gets quiet. Everything stays quiet a minute, and then Gran'mon starts singing back in the kitchen.

"Why did you bring your book home?" Mama says.

"Miss Hebert say I can stay home if I want," I say. "We had us lesson already."

"You sure she said that?" Mama says.

"Uh-huh."

"I'm go'n ask her, you know."

"She said it," I say.

Mama don't say no more, but I know she still looking at me, but I don't look at her. Then Spot starts barking outside and everybody look that way. But nobody don't move. Spot keeps on barking, and I go to the door to see what he's barking at. I see Daddy coming up the walk. I pull the door and go back to the fireplace.

"Daddy coming, Mama," I say.

"Wait," Gran'mon says, coming out the kitchen. "Let me talk to that nigger. I'll give him a piece of my mind."

Gran'mon goes to the door and pushes it open. She stands in the door and I hear Daddy talking to Spot. Then Daddy comes up to the gallery.

"Amy in there, Mama?" Daddy says.

"She is," Gran'mon says.

I hear Daddy coming up the steps.

"And where you think you going?" Gran'mon asks.

"I want to speak to her," Daddy says.

"Well, she don't want to speak to you," Gran'mon

says. "So you might 's well go right on back down them steps and march right straight out of my yard."

"I want speak to my wife," Daddy says.

"She ain't your wife no more," Gran'mon says. "She left you."

"What you mean she left me?" Daddy says.

"She ain't up at your house no more, is she?" Gran'mon says. "That look like a good enough sign to me that she done left."

"Amy?" Daddy calls.

Mama don't answer him. She's looking down in the fire. I don't feel good when Mama's looking like that.

"Amy?" Daddy calls.

Mama still don't answer him.

"You satisfied?" Gran'mon says.

"You the one trying to make Amy leave me," Daddy says. "You ain't never liked me—from the starting."

"That's right, I never did," Gran'mon says. "You yellow, you got a gap 'tween your teeth, and you ain't no good. You want me to say more?"

"You always wanted her to marry somebody else," Daddy says.

"You right again," Gran'mon says.

"Amy?" Daddy calls. "Can you hear me, honey?"

"She can hear you," Gran'mon says. "She's standing right there by that fireplace. She can hear you good 's I can hear you, and nigger, I can hear you too good for comfort."

"I'm going in there," Daddy says. "She got somebody in there and I'm going in there and see."

"You just take one more step toward my door," Gran'mon says, "and it'll take a' undertaker to get you out of here. So help me, God, I'll get that butcher knife out of that kitchen and chop on your tail till I can't see tail to chop on. You the kind of nigger like to rip and run up and down the road in your car long's you got a dime, but when you get broke and your belly get empty, you run to your wife and cry on her shoulder. You just take one more step toward this door, and I bet you somebody'll be crying at your funeral. If you know anybody who care that much for you, you old yellow dog."

Daddy is quiet a while, and then I hear him crying. I don't feel good, because I don't like to hear Daddy and Mama crying. I look at Mama, but she's looking down in the fire.

"You never liked me," Daddy says.

"You said that before," Gran'mon says. "And I repeat, no, I never liked you, don't like you, and never will like you. Now get out my yard 'fore I put the dog on you."

"I want see my boy," Daddy says, "I got a right to see my boy."

"In the first place, you ain't got no right in my yard," Gran'mon says.

"I want see my boy," Daddy says. "You might be able to keep me from seeing my wife, but you and nobody else can keep me from seeing my son. Half of him is me and I want see my—I want see him."

"You ain't leaving?" Gran'mon asks Daddy.

"I want see my boy," Daddy says. "And I'm go'n see my boy."

"Wait," Gran'mon says. "Your head hard. Wait till I come back. You go'n see all kind of boys."

Gran'mon comes back inside and goes to Uncle Al's room. I look toward the wall and I can hear Daddy moving on the gallery. I hear Mama crying and I look at her. I don't want see my mama crying, and I lay my head on Uncle Al's knee and I want cry, too.

"Amy, honey," Daddy calls, "ain't you coming up home and cook me something to eat? It's lonely up there without you, honey. You don't know how lonely it is without you. I can't stay up there without you, honey. Please come home."

I hear Gran'mon coming out of Uncle Al's room and I look at her. Gran'mon's got Uncle Al's shotgun and she's putting a shell in it.

"Mama?" Mama screams.

"Don't worry," Gran'mon says. "I'm just go'n shoot over his head. I ain't go'n have them sending me to the pen for a good-for-nothing nigger like that."

"Mama, don't," Mama says. "He might hurt himself."

"Good," Gran'mon says. "Save me the trouble of doing it for him."

Mama runs to the wall. "Eddie, run," she screams. "Mama got the shotgun."

I hear Daddy going down the steps. I hear Spot running after him barking. Gran'mon knocks the door open with the gun barrel and shoot. I hear Daddy hollering.

"Mama, you didn't?" Mama says.

"I shot two miles over that nigger's head," Gran'mon says. "Long-legged coward."

We all run out on the gallery, and I see Daddy out in the road crying. I can see the people coming

out on the galleries. They looking at us and they looking at Daddy. Daddy's standing out in the road crying.

"Boy, I would've like to seen old Eddie getting out of this yard," Uncle Al says.

Daddy's walking up and down the road in front of the house, and he's crying.

"Let's go back inside," Gran'mon says. "We won't be bothered with him for a while."

It's cold, and we all go back to the fire. Mama starts crying and goes back in the kitchen, and Mr. Freddie Jackson goes back there, too. Gran'mon's in Uncle Al's room putting up the gun, and I can hear her singing round there. She comes back in this side singing. She looks at the front door again, but she goes back in the kitchen where Mama and Mr. Freddie Jackson's at. I hear Mr. Freddie Jackson talking. Mama ain't saying nothing; she's still crying.

"Gran'mon shot Daddy?" I ask Uncle Al.

"Just scared him little bit," Uncle Al says.

Uncle Al pulls me between his knees. I look at the fire.

"Like your daddy, don't you?" Uncle Al says.

"Uh-huh."

"Your daddy's all right," Uncle Al says. "Little

foolish when it comes to cars, but he's all right."

"I don't like Mr. Freddie Jackson," I say.

"How come?" Uncle Al says.

"I don't like for him to stand close to my mama," I say. "Every time I look, he trying to stand close to my mama. My daddy suppose to stand close to my mama."

"You want go back home and be with your daddy?" Uncle Al asks.

"Uh-huh," I say. "But me and Mama go'n stay here now. I'm go'n sleep with you."

"But you rather go home and sleep in your own bed, huh?"

"Yes," I say. "I pull the cover 'way over my head. I like to sleep under the cover."

"You sleep like that all the time?" Uncle Al asks.

"Uh-huh."

"Even in the summertime, too?" Uncle Al says.

"Uh-huh," I say.

"Don't you ever get too warm?" Uncle Al says.

"Uh-uh," I say. "I feel good 'way under there."

Uncle Al rubs my head and I look down in the fire.

"Y'all come on in the kitchen and eat," Gran'mon calls.

Me and Uncle Al go back in the kitchen, and I see Mama and Mr. Freddie Jackson sitting at the table. Mama's got her head bowed. She raises her head and looks at me. I can see where she's been crying. She gets up from the table.

"You ate nothing all day," Gran'mon says. "Ain't you go'n eat?"

"I'm not hungry," Mama says.

"That's right, starve yourself," Gran'mon says. "See if that yellow thing out there care. Freddie?"

"I ate just 'fore I came over," he says.

They go in the front to sit at the fire. Gran'mon brings me and Uncle Al's food to the table. Uncle Al looks at me and we bow us heads.

"Thank Thee, Father, for this food Thou has given us," Uncle Al says.

I raise my head and start eating. We having spaghetti for dinner. I pick up a string of spaghetti and suck it up in my mouth. I make it go *loo-loo-loo-loo-loo-loo-loop*. Uncle Al looks at me and laugh. I do it again, and Uncle Al laughs again.

"Don't play with my food," Gran'mon says. "Eat it right."

Gran'mon is standing 'side the stove looking at me. I don't like old Gran'mon. Shooting at my daddy—I don't like her.

"Taste good?" Uncle Al asks.

"Uh-huh," I say.

Uncle Al winks at me and wraps his spaghetti on his fork and sticks it in his mouth. I try to wrap mine on my fork, but it keeps falling off. I can just pick up one at a time.

Gran'mon starts singing her song again. She fools round the stove a little while, and then she goes in the front room. I get a string of spaghetti and suck it up in my mouth. When I hear her coming back, I stop and eat right.

"Still out there," she says. "Sitting on that ditch bank crying like a baby. Let him cry. But he better not come back in this yard."

Gran'mon goes over to the stove and sticks a piece of wood in the fire. She starts singing again:

> *Oh, I'll be there,*
> *I'll be there,*
> *When the roll is called in Heaven, I'll be there.*

When Uncle Al finish eating, he gets himself a cup of coffee. Then he comes back to the table and sits down. He takes a good swallow of coffee and says, "Ahhhh. Want some?"

"I done told you before I don't want you giving that boy that coffee," Gran'mon says.

"I want poo-poo, Uncle Al," I say.

"Put your coat on," he says.

I go in the front room to get my coat, and I see Mama and Mr. Freddie Jackson sitting at the fireplace warming. I go back in the kitchen so Uncle Al can button my coat up for me. Then I go back in the front room again. Mama looks at me and ask me where I'm going.

"Toilet," I say.

"When you finish, you come on back in here," she says.

I go out on the gallery, and I see Daddy sitting on the ditch bank 'side the road. I don't say nothing to Daddy, I go on round the house. The grass is dry like hay. There ain't a leaf in that pecan tree—but I see a bird up there, and the wind 's moving the bird's feathers. I bet you that little bird 's some cold. I'm glad I'm not a bird. No daddy, no mama—I'm glad I'm not a bird.

I go in the toilet and look around, but I don't see no frogs or nothing. I get up on the seat and pull down my pants, then I squat over the hole. I can feel the wind coming up through the hole on me and I hurry up before I get too cold.

When I finish my poo-poo, I use a piece of paper out the catalog. Then I jump down off the seat and spit down in the hole the way I see Daddy do. I look up at the top for some spiders, but I don't see none. We got two spiders in us toilet at home. Gran'mon must be done killed all her spiders with Flit.

I push the door open and go back to the house. When I come round the gallery I see Daddy standing at the gate looking in the yard. He sees me.

"Sonny?" he calls.

"Hanh?"

"Come here, baby," he says.

I look toward the door, but I don't see nobody and I go to the gate where Daddy is. Daddy pushes the gate open and grabs me and hugs me to him.

"You still love your daddy, Sonny?" he asks.

"Uh-huh," I say.

Daddy hugs me and kisses me on the face.

"I love my baby," he says. "I love my baby. Where your mama?"

"Sitting at the fireplace warming," I say. "Mr. Freddie Jackson sitting there warming, too."

Daddy pushes me away real quickly and looks in my face.

"Who else sitting there warming?" he asks. "Who?"

"Just them," I say. "Uncle Al's drinking coffee at the table. Gran'mon's standing 'side the stove warming."

Daddy looks toward the house.

"This the last straw," he says. "I'm turning your Gran'mon in this minute. And you go'n be my witness. Come on."

"Where we going?" I ask.

"To that preacher's house," Daddy says. "And if he can't help me, I'm going back in the field to Madame Toussaint."

Daddy grabs my hand and me and him go up the quarter. I can see all the children going back to school.

"Step it up, Sonny," Daddy says.

"I'm coming fast as I can," I say.

"I'll see about that," Daddy says. "I'll see about that."

When me and Daddy get to Reverend Simmons's house, we go up on the gallery and Daddy knocks on the door. Mrs. Carey comes to the door to see what we want.

"Mrs. Carey, is the Reverend in?" Daddy asks.

"Yes," Mrs. Carey says. "Come on in."

Me and Daddy go inside and I see Reverend Simmons sitting at the fireplace. Reverend Simmons got on his eyeglasses and he's reading the Bible. He turns and looks at us when we come in. He takes off his glasses like he can't see us too good with them on, and he looks at us again. Mrs. Carey goes back in the kitchen, and me and Daddy go over to the fireplace.

"Good evening, Reverend," Daddy says.

"Good evening," Reverend Simmons says. "Hi, Sonny."

"Hi," I say.

"Reverend, I hate busting in on you like this, but I need your help," Daddy says. "Reverend, Amy done left me and her mama got her down at her house with another man and—"

"Now, calm down a second," Reverend Simmons says. He looks toward the kitchen. "Carey, bring Mr. Howard and Sonny a chair."

Mrs. Carey brings the chairs and goes right on back in the kitchen again. Daddy turns his chair so he can be facing Reverend Simmons.

"I come in pretty late last night 'cause my car broke down on me and I had to walk all the way— from the other side of Morgan up there," Daddy says. "When I get home, me and Amy get in a little squabble. This morning we squabble again, but I don't think too much of it. You know a man and a woman go'n have their little squabbles every once in a while. I go to work in the field. Work like a dog. Cutting cane right and left—trying to make up lost time I spent at the house this morning. When I come home for dinner—hungry's a dog—my wife, neither my boy, is there. No dinner—and I'm hungry's a dog. I go in the front room and all their clothes gone. Lord, I almost go crazy. I don't know what to do. I run out the house because I think she still mad at me and done gone down to her mama. I go down there and ask for her, and first thing I know here come Mama Rachel shooting at me with Uncle Al's shotgun."

"I can't believe that," Reverend Simmons says.

"If I'm telling a lie, I hope to never rise from this chair," Daddy says. "And I reckon she would've got me if I wasn't moving fast."

"That don't sound like Sister Rachel," Reverend Simmons says.

"Sound like her or don't sound like her, she did it," Daddy says. "Sonny right over there. He seen every bit of it. Ask him."

Reverend Simmons looks at me, but he don't ask me nothing. He just clicks his tongue and shakes his head.

"That don't sound like Sister Rachel," he says. "But if you say that's what she did, I'll go down there and talk to her."

"And that ain't all," Daddy says.

Reverend Simmons waits for Daddy to go on.

"She got Freddie Jackson in there with Amy, too," Daddy says.

Reverend Simmons looks at me and Daddy, then he goes over and gets his coat and hat from against the wall. Reverend Simmons's coat is long and black. His hat is big like a cowboy's hat.

"I'll be down the quarter, Carey," he tells Mrs. Simmons. "Be back quick as I can."

We go out of the house and Daddy holds my hand. Me and him and Reverend Simmons go out in the road and head on back down the quarter.

"Reverend Simmons, I want my wife back," Daddy says. "A man can't live by himself in this world. It too cold and cruel."

Reverend Simmons don't say nothing to Daddy. He starts humming a little song to himself. Reverend Simmons is big and he can walk fast. He takes big old long steps and me and Daddy got to walk fast to keep up with him. I got to run because Daddy's got my hand.

We get to Gran'mon's house and Reverend Simmons pushes the gate open and goes in the yard.

"Me and Sonny'll stay out here," Daddy says.

"I'm cold, Daddy," I say.

"I'll build a fire," Daddy says. "You want me build me and you a little fire?"

"Uh-huh."

"Help me get some sticks, then," Daddy says.

Me and Daddy get some grass and weeds and Daddy finds a big chunk of dry wood. We pile it all up and Daddy gets a match out his pocket and lights the fire.

"Feel better?" he says.

"Uh-huh."

"How come you not in school this evening?" Daddy asks.

"I wee-weed on myself," I say.

I tell Daddy because I know Daddy ain't go'n whip me.

"You peed on yourself at school?" Daddy asks. "Sonny, I thought you was a big boy. That's something little babies do."

"Miss Hebert want see you and Mama," I say.

"I don't have time to see nobody now," Daddy

says. "I got my own troubles. I just hope that preacher in there can do something."

I look up at Daddy, but he's looking down in the fire.

"Sonny?" I hear Mama calling me.

I turn and I see Mama and all of them standing out there on the gallery.

"Hanh?" I answer.

"Come in here before you catch a death of cold," Mama says.

Daddy goes to the fence and looks across the pickets at Mama.

"Amy," he says, "please come home. I swear I ain't go'n do it no more."

"Sonny, you hear me talking to you?" Mama calls.

"I ain't go'n catch cold," I say. "We got a fire. I'm warm."

"Amy, please come home," Daddy says. "Please, honey. I forgive you. I forgive Mama. I forgive everybody. Just come home."

I look at Mama and Reverend Simmons talking on the gallery. The others ain't talking; they just standing there looking out in the road at me and Daddy. Reverend Simmons comes out the yard and over to the fire. Daddy comes to the fire where me and Reverend Simmons is. He looks at Reverend Simmons but Reverend Simmons won't look back at him.

"Well, Reverend?" Daddy says.

"She say she tired of you and that car," Reverend Simmons says.

Daddy falls down on the ground and cries.

"A man just can't live by himself in this cold, cruel world," he says. "He got to have a woman to stand by him. He just can't make it by himself. God, help me."

"Be strong, man," Reverend Simmons says.

"I can't be strong with my wife in there and me out here," Daddy says. "I need my wife."

"Well, you go'n have to straighten that out the best way you can," Reverend Simmons says. "And I talked to Sister Rachel. She said she didn't shoot to hurt you. She just shot to kind of scare you away."

"She didn't shoot to hurt me?" Daddy says. "And I reckon them things was jelly beans I heard zooming three inches over my head?"

"She said she didn't shoot to hurt you," Reverend Simmons says. He holds his hands over the fire. "This fire's good, but I got to get back up the quarter. Got to get my wood for tonight. I'll see you people later. And I hope everything comes out all right."

"Reverend, you sure you can't do nothing?" Daddy asks.

"I tried, son," Reverend Simmons says. "Now we'll leave it in God's hand."

"But I want my wife back now," Daddy says. "God take so long to—"

"Mr. Howard, that's blasphemous," Reverend Simmons says.

"I don't want blaspheme Him," Daddy says. "But I'm in a mess. I'm in a big mess. I want my wife."

"I'd suggest you kneel down sometime," Reverend Simmons says. "That always helps in a family."

Reverend Simmons looks at me like he's feeling sorry for me, then he goes on back up the quarter. I can see his coattail hitting him round the knees.

"You coming in this yard, Sonny?" Mama calls.

"I'm with Daddy," I say.

Mama goes back in the house, and Gran'mon and them follow her.

"When you want one of them preachers to do something for you, they can't do a doggone thing," Daddy says. "Nothing but stand up in that churchhouse and preach 'bout Heaven. I hate to go to that old hoo-doo woman, but I reckon there ain't nothing else I can do. You want go back there with me, Sonny?"

"Uh-huh."

"Come on," Daddy says.

Daddy takes my hand and me and him leave the fire. When I get 'way down the quarter, I look back and see the fire still burning. We cross the railroad tracks and I can see the people cutting cane. They got plenty cane all on the ground.

"Get me piece of cane, Daddy," I say.

"Sonny, please," Daddy says. "I'm thinking."

"I want piece of two-ninety," I say.

Daddy turns my hand loose and jumps over the ditch. He finds a piece of two-ninety and jumps back over. Daddy takes out a little pocketknife and peels the cane. He gives me a round and he cut him off a round and chew it. I like two-ninety cane because it's soft and sweet and got plenty juice in it.

"I want another piece," I say.

Daddy cuts off another round and hands it to me.

"I'll be glad when you big enough to peel your own cane," he says.

"I can peel my own cane now," I say.

Daddy breaks off three joints and hands it to me.

I peel the cane with my teeth. Two-ninety cane is soft and it's easy to peel.

Me and Daddy go round the bend, and then I can see Madame Toussaint's house. Madame Toussaint's got a' old house, and look like it want to fall down any minute. I'm scared of Madame Toussaint. Billy Joe Martin say Madame Toussaint's a witch, and he say one time he seen Madame Toussaint riding a broom.

Daddy pulls Madame Toussaint's little old broken-down gate open and we go in the yard. Me and Daddy go far as the steps, but we don't go up on the gallery. Madame Toussaint's got plenty trees round her house, little trees and big trees. And she got plenty moss hanging on every tree. I see a pecan over there on the ground but I'm scared to go and pick it up. Madame Toussaint'll put a bad mark on me and I'll turn to a frog or something. I let Madame Toussaint's little old pecan stay right where it is. And I go up to Daddy and let him hold my hand.

"Madame Toussaint?" Daddy calls.

Madame Toussaint don't answer. Like she ain't there.

"Madame Toussaint?" Daddy calls again.

"Who that?" Madame Toussaint answers.

"Me," Daddy says. "Eddie Howard and his little boy, Sonny."

"What you want, Eddie Howard?" Madame Toussaint calls from in her house.

"I want talk to you," Daddy says. "I need little advice on something."

I hear a dog bark three times in the house. He must be a big old dog because he's sure got a heavy voice. Madame Toussaint comes to the door and cracks it open.

"Can I come in?" Daddy says.

"Come in, Eddie Howard," Madame Toussaint says.

Me and Daddy go up the steps and Madame Toussaint opens the door for us. Madame Toussaint's a little bitty little old woman and her face is brown like cowhide. I look at Madame Toussaint and I walk close 'side Daddy. Me and Daddy go in the house and Madame Toussaint shuts the door and comes back to her fireplace. She sits down in her big old rocking chair and looks at me and Daddy. I look round Daddy's leg at Madame Toussaint, but I let Daddy hold my hand. Madame Toussaint's house don't smell good. It's too dark in here. It don't smell good at all. Madame Toussaint ought to have a window or something open in her house.

"I need some advice, Madame Toussaint," Daddy says.

"Your wife left you," Madame Toussaint says.

"How you know?" Daddy asks.

"That's all you men come back here for," Madame Toussaint says. "That's how I know."

Daddy nods his head. "Yes," he says. "She done left me and staying with another man."

"She left," Madame Toussaint says. "But she's not staying with another man."

"Yes, she is," Daddy says.

"She's not," Madame Toussaint says. "You trying to tell me my business?"

"No, ma'am," Daddy says.

"I should hope not," Madame Toussaint says.

Madame Toussaint ain't got but three old rotten teeth in her mouth. I bet you she can't peel no cane with them old rotten teeth. I bet you they'd break off in a hard piece of cane.

"I need advice, Madame Toussaint," Daddy says.

"You got money?" Madame Toussaint asks.

"I got some," Daddy says.

"How much?" she asks Daddy. She's looking up at Daddy like she don't believe him.

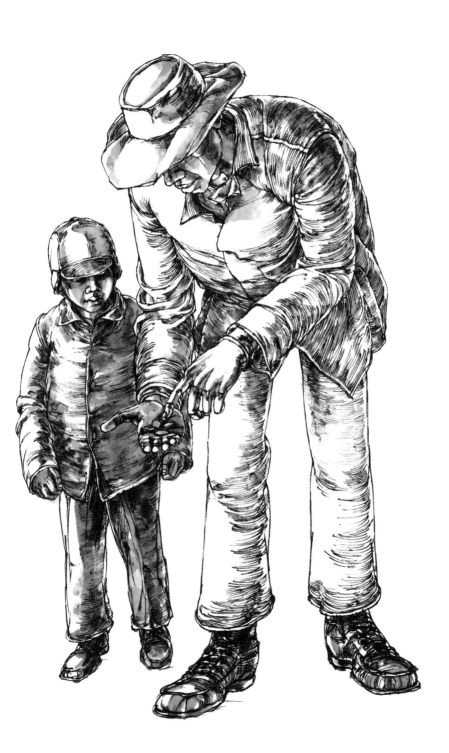

Daddy turns my hand loose and sticks his hand down in his pocket. He gets all his money out his pocket and leans over the fire to see how much he's got. I see some matches and piece of string and some nails in Daddy's hand. I reach for the piece of string and Daddy taps me on the hand with his other hand.

"I got about seventy-five cents," Daddy says. "Counting them pennies."

"My price is three dollars," Madame Toussaint says.

"I can cut you a load of wood," Daddy says. "Or make grocery for you. I'll do anything in the world if you can help me, Madame Toussaint."

"Three dollars," Madame Toussaint says. "I got all the wood I'll need this winter. Enough grocery to last me till summer."

"But this all I got," Daddy says.

"When you get more, come back," Madame Toussaint says.

"But I want my wife back now," Daddy says. "I can't wait till I get more money."

"Three dollars is my price," Madame Toussaint says. "No more, no less."

"But can't you give me just a little advice for seventy-five cents?" Daddy says. "Seventy-five cents worth? Maybe I can start from there and figure something out."

Madame Toussaint looks at me and looks at Daddy again.

"You say that's your boy?" she says.

"Yes, ma'am," Daddy says.

"Nice-looking boy," Madame Toussaint says.

"His name's Sonny," Daddy says.

"Hi, Sonny," Madame Toussaint says.

"Say 'Hi' to Madame Toussaint," Daddy says. "Go on."

"Hi," I say, sticking close to Daddy.

"Well, Madame Toussaint?" Daddy says.

"Give me the money," Madame Toussaint says. "Don't complain to me if you not satisfied."

"Don't worry," Daddy says. "I won't complain. Anything to get her back home."

Daddy leans over the fire again and picks the money out of his hand. Then he reaches it to Madame Toussaint.

"Give me that little piece of string," Madame Toussaint says. "It might come in handy sometime in the future. Wait," she says. "Run it 'cross the left side of the boy's face three times, then pass it to me behind your back."

"What's that for?" Daddy asks.

"Just do like I say," Madame Toussaint says.

"Yes, ma'am," Daddy says. Daddy turns to me. "Hold still, Sonny," he says. He rubs the little old dirty piece of cord over my face, and then he sticks his hand behind his back.

Madame Toussaint reaches in her pocket and takes out her pocketbook. She opens it and puts the money in. She opens another little compartment and stuffs the string down in it. Then she snaps the pocketbook and puts it back in her pocket. She picks up three little green sticks she got tied together and starts poking in the fire with them.

"What's the advice?" Daddy asks.

Madame Toussaint don't say nothing.

"Madame Toussaint?" Daddy says.

Madame Toussaint still don't answer him, she just looks down in the fire. Her face is red from the fire. I get scared of Madame Toussaint. She can ride all over the plantation on her broom. Billy Joe Martin say he seen her one night riding 'cross the houses. She was whipping her broom with three switches.

Madame Toussaint raises her head and looks at Daddy. Her eyes's big and white, and I get scared of her. I hide my face 'side Daddy's leg.

"Give it up," I hear her say.

"Give what up?" Daddy says.

"Give it up," she says.

"What?" Daddy says.

"Give it up," she says.

"I don't even know what you talking 'bout," Daddy says. "How can I give up something and I don't even know what it is?"

"I said it three times," Madame Toussaint says. "No more, no less. Up to you now to follow it through from there."

"Follow what from where?" Daddy says. "You said three little old words: 'Give it up.' I don't know no more now than I knowed 'fore I got here."

"I told you you wasn't go'n be satisfied," Madame Toussaint says.

"Satisfied?" Daddy says. "Satisfied for what? You gived me just three little old words and you want me to be satisfied?"

"You can leave," Madame Toussaint says.

"Leave?" Daddy says. "You mean I give you seventy-five cents for three words? A quarter a word? And I'm leaving? No, Lord."

"Rollo?" Madame Toussaint says.

I see Madame Toussaint's big old black dog get up

out of the corner and come where she is. Madame Toussaint pats the dog on the head with her hand.

"Two dollars and twenty-five cents more and you get all the advice you need," Madame Toussaint says.

"Can't I get you a load of wood and fix your house for you or something?" Daddy says.

"I don't want my house fixed and I don't need no more wood," Madame Toussaint says. "I got three loads of wood just three days ago from a man who didn't have money. Before I know it I'll have wood piled up all over my yard."

"Can't I do anything?" Daddy says.

"You can leave," Madame Toussaint says. "I ought to have somebody else dropping round pretty soon. Lately I've been having men dropping in three times a day. All of them just like you, in trouble with their wives. Get out my house before I put the dog on you. You been here too long for seventy-five cents."

Madame Toussaint's big old jet-black dog gives three loud barks that makes my head hurt. Madame Toussaint pats him on the back to calm him down.

"Come on, Sonny," Daddy says.

I let Daddy take my hand and we go over to the door.

"I still don't feel like you helped me very much,

though," Daddy says.

Madame Toussaint pats her big old jet-black dog on the head and she don't answer Daddy. Daddy pushes the door open and we go outside. It's some cold outside. Me and Daddy go down Madame Toussaint's old broken-down steps.

"What was them words?" Daddy asks me.

"Hanh?"

"What she said when she looked up out of that fire?" Daddy asks.

"I was scared," I say. "Her face was red and her eyes got big and white. I was scared. I had to hide my face."

"Didn't you hear what she told me?" Daddy asks.

"She told you three dollars," I say.

"I mean when she looked up," Daddy says.

"She say, 'Give it up,' " I say.

"Yes," Daddy says. " 'Give it up.' Give what up? I don't even know what she's talking 'bout. I hope she don't mean give you and Amy up. She ain't that crazy. I don't know nothing else she can be talking 'bout. You don't know, do you?"

"Uh-uh," I say.

" 'Give it up,' " Daddy says. "I don't even know what she's talking 'bout. I wonder who them other men was she was speaking of. Johnny and his wife had a fight the other week. It might be him. Frank Armstrong and his wife had a round couple weeks back. Could be him. I wish I knowed what she told them."

"I want another piece of cane," I say.

"No," Daddy says. "You'll be pee-ing in bed all night tonight."

"I'm go'n sleep with Uncle Al," I say. "Me and him go'n sleep in his bed."

"Please be quiet, Sonny," Daddy says. "I got enough troubles on my mind. Don't add more to it."

Me and Daddy walk in the middle of the road. Daddy holds my hand. I can hear a tractor—I see it across the field. The people loading cane on the trailer back of the tractor.

"Come on," Daddy says. "We going over to Frank Armstrong."

Daddy totes me 'cross the ditch on his back. I ride on Daddy's back and I look at the stubbles where the people done cut the cane. Them rows some long. Plenty cane's laying on the ground. I can see cane all over the field. Me and Daddy go over where the people cutting cane.

"How come you ain't working this evening?" a

man asks Daddy. The man's shucking a big armful of cane with his cane knife.

"Frank Armstrong round anywhere?" Daddy asks the man.

"Farther over," the man says. "Hi, youngster."

"Hi," I say.

Me and Daddy go 'cross the field. I look at the people cutting cane. That cane is some tall. I want another piece, but I might wee-wee in Uncle Al's bed.

Me and Daddy go over where Mr. Frank Armstrong and Mrs. Julie's cutting cane. Mrs. Julie got overalls on just like Mr. Frank got. She's even wearing one of Mr. Frank's old hats.

"How y'all?" Daddy says.

"So-so, and yourself?" Mrs. Julie says.

"I'm trying to make it," Daddy says. "Can I borrow your husband there a minute?"

"Sure," Mrs. Julie says. "But don't keep him too long. We trying to reach the end 'fore dark."

"It won't take long," Daddy says.

Mr. Frank and them got a little fire burning in one of the middles. Me and him and Daddy go over there. Daddy squats down and let me slide off his back.

"What's the trouble?" Mr. Frank asks Daddy.

"Amy left me, Frank," Daddy says.

Mr. Frank holds his hands over the fire.

"She left you?" he says.

"Yes," Daddy says. "And I want her back, Frank."

"What can I do?" Mr. Frank says. "She's no kin to me. I can't go and make her come back."

"I thought maybe you could tell me what you and Madame Toussaint talked about," Daddy says.

"That's if you don't mind, Frank."

"What?" Mr. Frank says. "Who told you I talked with Madame Toussaint?"

"Nobody," Daddy says. "But I heard you and Julie had a fight, and I thought maybe you went back to her for advice."

"For what?" Mr. Frank says.

"So you and Julie could make up," Daddy says.

"Well, I'll be damned," Mr. Frank says. "I done heard everything. Excuse me, Sonny. But your daddy's enough to make anybody cuss."

I look up at Daddy, and I look back in the fire again.

"Please, Frank," Daddy says. "I'm desperate. I'm ready to try anything. I'll do anything to get her back in my house."

"Why don't you just go and get her?" Mr. Frank says. "That makes sense."

"I can't," Daddy says. "Mama won't let me come in the yard. She even took a shot at me once today."

"What?" Mr. Frank says. He looks at Daddy, and then he just bust out laughing. Daddy laughs little bit, too.

"What y'all talked about, Frank?" Daddy asks. "Maybe if I try the same thing, maybe I'll be able to get her back, too."

Mr. Frank laughs at Daddy, then he stops and just looks at Daddy.

"My advice won't help your case, Eddie," he says.

"It might," Daddy says.

"It can't," Mr. Frank says. "First you got to get close to your wife, and your mother-in-law won't allow that. Anyhow, everybody's advice is different."

"Tell me what she told you, Frank," Daddy says. "Maybe I can use it for a starting point."

"She told me I had to listen to my wife little more," Mr. Frank says.

" 'Bout what?" Daddy says.

" 'Bout everything," Mr. Frank says. "Said I wasn't listening to her enough. Said I walked out the house too much when Julie was talking to me. Don't ask me how she knowed all that, but she knowed it. That old woman know everything back there."

"That's all she told you to do, just listen?" Daddy asks.

"She told me to pat her on the back sometime and make myself kiss her sometime. I told her Julie chewed tobacco. She said she knowed all that—kiss her anyhow. And sometime tell her the food is good. Don't ask me how she knowed all this, but she knowed it. Well, I do all she told me—'long with rubbing her foot every night."

Me and Daddy look at Mrs. Julie cutting cane. I can't see Mrs. Julie's foot.

"Rub her foot for what?" Daddy says.

"Her foot hurt her from standing up all day," Mr. Frank says. "How she knowed all this, only God

Ernest J. Gaines

knows. But she told me I had to rub Julie's foot—
'specially her big toe—that joint on the side there."

I look down at my shoe. I can't see my foot.

"You see when Julie was young, she sprained her
big toe and never had it corrected," Mr. Frank says.
"So it trouble her now when she stand up a lot. Said
for me to take little salve and rub it every night.
Don't quit just 'cause Julie start giggling. Giggling
like that just 'cause I don't rub her foot enough.
After I been doing it a while, she won't giggle at all.
How that old woman know all this, only God
knows."

"It worked?" Daddy asks.

"Getting along like two peas in a pod," Mr. Frank
says. "Every night after she wash her foot, I take little
salve and rub it for her. Done already stopped giggling. Less I kinda tickle her little bit with my finger.

"But what I'm telling you all this for?" Mr. Frank
says quickly. "That's private."

"It won't get no farther than right here," Daddy
says. "You right, though, it can't help me. Amy don't
even have no foot trouble."

"She will when she gets older," Mr. Frank says.
"Well, I got to get back to work. What you go'n do
now?"

"I don't know," Daddy says. "If I had three dollars she'd give me some advice. But I don't have a red copper. You wouldn't have three dollars you could spare till payday, huh?"

"I don't have a dime," Mr. Frank says. "Since we made up, Julie keeps most of the money."

"You think she'd lend me three dollars till Saturday?" Daddy asks.

"I don't know if she got that much on her," Mr. Frank says. "I'll go over and ask her."

I watch Mr. Frank going 'cross the rows where Mrs. Julie's cutting cane. They start talking, and then I hear them laughing.

"You warm?" Daddy asks.

"Uh-huh."

I see Mr. Frank coming back to the fire.

"She don't have it on her, but she got it at the house," Mr. Frank says. "If you can wait till we knock off."

"No," Daddy says. "I can't wait till night. I got to try to borrow it from somebody now."

"Why don't you go 'cross the field and try Johnny Green?" Mr. Frank says. "He's always got some money. Maybe he'll lend it to you."

"I'll ask him," Daddy says. "Get on, Sonny."

Me and Daddy go back 'cross the field. I can hear Mr. Johnny Green singing, and Daddy turns that way and we go down where Mr. Johnny is. Mr. Johnny stops his singing when he sees me and Daddy. He chops the top off a' armful of cane and throws it 'cross the row. Mr. Johnny's cutting cane all by himself.

"Hi, Brother Howard," Mr. Johnny says.

"Hi," Daddy says. Daddy squats down and let me slide off.

"Hi there, little Brother Sonny," Mr. Johnny says.

"Hi," I say.

"How you?" Mr. Johnny asks.

"I'm all right," I say.

"That's good," Mr. Johnny says. "And how you this beautiful God-sent day, Brother Howard?"

"I'm fine," Daddy says. "Johnny, I want to know if you can spare me 'bout three dollars till Saturday?"

"Sure, Brother Howard," Mr. Johnny says. "You mind telling me just why you need it? I don't mind lending a good brother anything, long's I know he ain't wasting it on women or drink."

"I want pay Madame Toussaint for some advice," Daddy says.

"Little trouble, Brother?" Mr. Johnny asks.

"Amy done left me, Johnny," Daddy says. "I need some advice. I just got to get her back."

"I know what you mean, Brother," Mr. Johnny says. "I had to visit Madame—you won't carry this no farther, huh?"

"No," Daddy says.

"Couple months ago I had to take a little trip back there to see her," Mr. Johnny says. "Little misunderstanding between me and Sister Laura."

"She helped?" Daddy asks.

"Told me to stop spending so much time in church and little more time at home," Mr. Johnny says. "I couldn't see that. You know, far back as I can go in my family my people been good church members."

"I know that," Daddy says.

"My pappy was a deacon and my mammy didn't miss a Sunday long as I can remember," Mr. Johnny says. "And that's how I was raised. To fear God. I just couldn't see it when she first told me that. But I thought it over. I went for a long walk back in the field. I got down on my knees and looked up at the sky. I asked God to show me the way—to tell me what to do. And He did, He surely did. He told me to do just like Madame Toussaint said. Slack up going to church. Go twice a week, but spend the rest of the time with her. Just like that He told me. And I'm doing exactly what He said. Twice a week. And, Brother Howard, don't spread this round, but there might be a little Johnny next summer sometime."

"No?" Daddy says.

"Uhnnnn-hunh," Mr. Johnny says.

"I'll be doggone," Daddy says. "I'm glad to hear that."

"I'll be the happiest man on this whole plantation," Mr. Johnny says.

"I know how you feel," Daddy says. "Yes, I know how you feel. But that three, can you lend it to me?"

"Sure, Brother," Mr. Johnny says. "Anything to bring a family back together. Nothing more important in this world than family love. Yes, indeed."

Mr. Johnny unbuttons his top overalls pocket and takes out a dollar.

"Only thing I got is five, Brother Howard," he says. "You wouldn't happen to have some change, would you?"

"I don't have a red copper," Daddy says. "But I'll be more than happy if you can let me have that five. I need some grocery in the house, too."

"Sure, Brother," Mr. Johnny says. He hands

Daddy the dollar. "Nothing looks more beautiful than a family at a table eating something the little woman just cooked. But you did say Saturday, didn't you, Brother?"

"Yes," Daddy says. "I'll pay you back soon 's I get paid. You can't ever guess how much this means to me, Johnny."

"Glad I can help, Brother," Mr. Johnny says. "Hope she can do likewise."

"I hope so too," Daddy says. "Anyhow, this a start."

"See you Saturday, Brother," Mr. Johnny says.

"Soon 's I get paid," Daddy says. "Hop on, Sonny, and hold tight. We going back."

IV

Daddy walks up on Madame Toussaint's gallery and knocks on the door.

"Who that?" Madame Toussaint asks.

"Me. Eddie Howard," Daddy says. He squats down so I can slide off his back. I slide down and let Daddy hold my hand.

"What you want, Eddie Howard?" Madame Toussaint asks.

"I got three dollars," Daddy says. "I still want that advice."

Madame Toussaint's big old jet-black dog barks three times, and then I hear Madame Toussaint coming to the door. She peeps through the keyhole at me and Daddy. She opens the door and let me and Daddy come in. We go to the fireplace and warm. Madame Toussaint comes to the fireplace and sits down in her big old rocking chair. She looks up at Daddy. I look for big old Rollo, but I don't see him. He must be under the bed or hiding somewhere in the corner.

"You got three dollars?" Madame Toussaint asks Daddy.

"Yes," Daddy says. He takes out the dollar and shows it to Madame Toussaint.

Madame Toussaint holds her hand up for it.

"This is five," Daddy says. "I want two back."

"You go'n get your two," Madame Toussaint says.

"Come to think of it," Daddy says, "I ought to just owe you two and a quarter, since I done already gived you seventy-five cents."

"You want advice?" Madame Toussaint asks Daddy.

Madame Toussaint looks like she's getting mad with Daddy now.

"Sure," Daddy says. "But since—"

"Then shut up and hand me your money," Madame Toussaint says.

"But I done already—" Daddy says.

"Get out my house, nigger," Madame Toussaint says. "And don't come back till you learn how to act."

"All right," Daddy says, "I'll give you three more dollars."

He hands Madame Toussaint the dollar.

Madame Toussaint gets her pocketbook out her pocket. Then she leans close to the fire so she can look down in it. She sticks her hand in the pocketbook and gets two dollars. She looks at the two dollars a long time. She stands up and gets her eyeglasses off the mantelpiece and puts them on her eyes. She looks at the two dollars a long time, then she hands them to Daddy. She sticks the dollar bill Daddy gived her in the pocketbook, then she takes her eyeglasses off and puts them back on the mantelpiece. Madame Toussaint sits in her big old rocking chair and starts poking in the fire with the three sticks again. Her face gets red from the fire, her eyes get big and white. I turn my head and hide behind Daddy's leg.

"Go set fire to your car," Madame Toussaint says.

"What?" Daddy says.

"Go set fire to your car," Madame Toussaint says.

"You talking to me?" Daddy says.

"Go set fire to your car," Madame Toussaint says.

"Now, just a minute," Daddy says. "I didn't give you my hard-earned three dollars for that kind of foolishness. I dismiss that seventy-five cents you took from me, but not my three dollars that easy."

"You want your wife back?" Madame Toussaint asks Daddy.

"That's what I'm paying you for," Daddy says.

"Then go set fire to your car," Madame Toussaint says. "You can't have both."

"You must be fooling," Daddy says.

"I don't fool," Madame Toussaint says. "You paid for advice and I'm giving you advice."

"You mean that?" Daddy says. "You mean I got to go burn up my car for Amy to come back home?"

"If you want her back there," Madame Toussaint says. "Do you?"

"I wouldn't be standing here if I didn't," Daddy says.

"Then go and burn it up," Madame Toussaint says. "A gallon of coal oil and a penny box of match ought to do the trick. You got any gas in it?"

"A little bit—if nobody ain't drained it," Daddy says.

"Then you can use that," Madame Toussaint says. "But if you want her back there, you got to burn it up. That's my advice to you. And if I was you, I'd do it right away. You can never tell."

"Tell about what?" Daddy asks.

"She might be with another man a week from now," Madame Toussaint says. "This man loves her and he's kind. And that's what a woman wants. That's what they need. You men don't know this, but you better learn it before it's too late."

"What's the other man's name?" Daddy asks. "Can it be Freddie Jackson?"

"It can," Madame Toussaint says. "But it don't have to be. Any man that'd give her love and kindness."

"I love her," Daddy says. "I give her kindness. I'm always giving her love and kindness."

"When you home, you mean," Madame Toussaint says. "How about when you running up and down the road in your car? How do you think she feels then?"

Daddy don't say nothing.

"You men better learn," Madame Toussaint says.

"Now, if you want her, go and burn it. If you don't want her, go and get drunk off them two dollars and sleep in a cold bed tonight."

"You mean she'll come back tonight?" Daddy asks.

"She's ready to come back right now," Madame Toussaint says. "Poor little thing."

I look round Daddy's leg at Madame Toussaint. Madame Toussaint's looking in the fire. Her face ain't red no more; her eyes ain't big and white, either.

"She's not happy where she is," Madame Toussaint says.

"She's with her mama," Daddy says.

"You don't have to tell me my business," Madame Toussaint says. "I know where she is. And I still say she's not happy. She much rather be back in her own house. Women like to be in their own house. That's their world. You men done messed up the outside world so bad that they feel lost and out of place in it. Her house is her world. Only there she can do what she want. She can't do that in anybody else house—mama or nobody else. But you men don't know any of this. Y'all never know a woman feels, because you never ask how she feels. Long 's she there when you get there you satisfied.

Long 's you give her two or three dollars every week-end you think she ought to be satisfied. But keep on. One day all of you'll find out."

"Couldn't I sell the car or something?" Daddy asks.

"You got to burn it," Madame Toussaint says. "How come your head so hard?"

"But I paid good money for that car," Daddy says. "It wouldn't look right if I just jumped up and put fire to it."

"You, get out my house," Madame Toussaint says, pointing her finger at Daddy. "Go do what you want with your car. It's yours. But just don't come back here bothering me for no more advice."

"I don't know," Daddy says.

"I'm through talking," Madame Toussaint says. "Rollo? Come here, baby."

Big old jet-black Rollo comes up and puts his head in Madame Toussaint's lap. Madame Toussaint pats him on the head.

"That's what I got to do, hanh?" Daddy says.

Madame Toussaint don't answer Daddy. She starts singing a song to Rollo:

> *Mama's little baby,*
> *Mama's little baby.*

"He bad?" Daddy asks.

> *Mama's little baby,*
> *Mama's little baby.*

"Do he bite?" Daddy asks.
Madame Toussaint keeps on singing:

> *Mama's little baby,*
> *Mama's little baby.*

"Come on," Daddy says. "I reckon we better be going."

Daddy squats down and I climb up on his back. I look down at Madame Toussaint patting big old jet-black Rollo on his head.

Daddy pushes the door open and we go outside. It's cold outside. Daddy goes down Madame Toussaint's three old broken-down steps and we go out in the road.

"I don't know," Daddy says.

"Hanh?"

"I'm talking to myself," Daddy says. "I don't know about burning up my car."

"You go'n burn up your car?" I ask.

"That's what Madame Toussaint say to do," Daddy says.

"You ain't go'n have no more car?"

"I reckon not," Daddy says. "You want me and Mama to stay together?"

"Uh-huh."

"Then I reckon I got to burn it up," Daddy says. "But I sure hope there was another way out. I put better than three hundred dollars in that car."

Daddy walks fast and I bounce on his back.

"God, I wish there was another way out," Daddy says. "Don't look like that's right for a man to just jump up and set fire to something like that. What you think I ought to do?"

"Hanh?"

"Go back to sleep," Daddy says. "I don't know what I'm educating you for."

"I ain't sleeping," I say.

"I don't know," Daddy says. "That don't look right. All Frank Armstrong had to do was put salve on Julie's big toe every night. All Johnny had to do was stop going to church so much. Neither one of them had to burn nothing down. Johnny didn't have to burn down the church; Frank Armstrong didn't have to burn down his house; not even a pair of pants. But me, I got to burn up my car. Charged us all the same thing—no, even charged me seventy-five cents more—and I got to burn up a car I can still get some use out. Now, that don't sound right, do it?''

''Hanh?''

''I can't figure it,'' Daddy says. ''Look like I ought to be able to sell it for little something. Get some of my money back. Burning it, I don't get a red copper. That just don't sound right to me. I wonder if she was fooling. No. She say she wasn't. But maybe that wasn't my advice she seen in that fireplace. Maybe that was somebody else advice. Maybe she gived me the wrong one. Maybe it belongs to the man coming back there after me. They go there three times a day, she can get them mixed up.''

''I'm scared of Madame Toussaint, Daddy,'' I say.

''Must've been somebody else,'' Daddy says. ''I bet it was. I bet you anything it was.''

I bounce on Daddy's back and I close my eyes. I open them and I see me and Daddy going 'cross the railroad tracks. We go up the quarter to Gran'mon's house. Daddy squats down and I slide off his back.

''Run in the house to the fire,'' Daddy says. ''Tell your mama come to the door.''

Soon 's I come in the yard, Spot runs down the walk and starts barking. Mama and all of them come out on the gallery.

"My baby," Mama says. Mama comes down the steps and hugs me to her. "My baby," she says.

"Look at that old yellow thing standing out in that road," Gran'mon says. "What you ought to been done was got the sheriff on him for kidnap."

Me and Mama go back on the gallery.

"I been to Madame Toussaint's house," I say.

Mama looks at me and looks at Daddy out in the road. Daddy comes to the gate and looks at us on the gallery.

"Amy?" Daddy calls. "Can I speak to you a minute? Just one minute?"

"You don't get away from my gate, I'm go'n make that shotgun speak to you," Gran'mon says. "I didn't get you at twelve o'clock, but I won't miss you now."

"Amy, honey," Daddy calls. "Please."

"Come on, Sonny," Mama says.

"Where you going?" Gran'mon asks.

"Far as the gate," Mama says. "I'll talk to him. I reckon I owe him that much."

"You leave this house with that nigger, don't ever come back here again," Gran'mon says.

"You oughtn't talk like that, Rachel," Uncle Al says.

"I talk like I want," Gran'mon says. "She's my daughter; not yours, neither his."

Me and Mama go out to the gate where Daddy is. Daddy stands outside the gate and me and Mama stand inside.

"Lord, you look good, Amy," Daddy says. "Honey, didn't you miss me? Go on and say it. Go on and say how bad you missed me."

"That's all you want to say to me?" Mama says.

"Honey, please," Daddy says. "Say you missed me. I been grieving all day like a dog."

"Come on, Sonny," Mama says. "Let's go back inside."

"Honey," Daddy says. "Please don't turn your back on me and go back to Freddie Jackson. Honey, I love you. I swear 'fore God I love you. Honey, you listening?"

"Come on, Sonny," Mama says.

"Honey," Daddy says, "if I burn the car like Madame Toussaint say, you'll come back home?"

"What?" Mama says.

"She say for Daddy—"

"Be still, Sonny," Mama says.

"She told me to set fire to it and you'll come back home," Daddy says. "You'll come back, honey?"

"She told you to burn up your car?" Mama says.

"If I want you to come back," Daddy says. "If I do it, you'll come back?"

"If you burn it up," Mama says. "If you burn it up, yes, I'll come back."

"Tonight?" Daddy says.

"Yes; tonight," Mama says.

"If I sold it?" Daddy says.

"Burn it," Mama says.

"I can get about fifty for it," Daddy says. "You could get couple dresses out of that."

"Burn it," Mama says. "You know what burn is?"

Daddy looks across the gate at Mama, and Mama looks right back at him. Daddy nods his head.

"I can't argue with you, honey," he says. "I'll go and burn it right now. You can come see if you want."

"No," Mama says, "I'll be here when you come back."

"Couldn't you go up home and start cooking some supper?" Daddy asks. "I'm just 's hungry as a dog."

"I'll cook when that car is burnt," Mama says. "Come on, Sonny."

"Can I go see Daddy burn his car, Mama?" I ask.

"No," Mama says. "You been in that cold long enough."

"I want see Daddy burn his car," I say. I start crying and stomping so Mama'll let me go.

"Let him go, honey," Daddy says. "I'll keep him warm."

"You can go," Mama says. "But don't come to me if you start that coughing tonight, you hear?"

"Uh-huh," I say.

Mama makes sure all my clothes's buttoned good, then she let me go. I run out in the road where Daddy is.

"I'll be back soon 's I can, honey," Daddy says. "And we'll straighten out everything, hear?"

"Just make sure you burn it," Mama says. "I'll find out."

"Honey, I'm go'n burn every bit of it," Daddy says.

"I'll be here when you come back," Mama says. "How you figuring on getting up there?"

"I'll go over and see if George Williams can't take me," Daddy says.

"I don't want Sonny in that cold too long," Mama says. "And you keep your hands in your pockets, Sonny."

"I ain't go'n take them out," I say.

Mama goes back up the walk toward the house. Daddy stands there just watching her.

"Lord, that's a sweet little woman," he says, shaking his head. "That's a sweet little woman you see going back to that house."

"Come on, Daddy," I say. "Let's go burn up the car."

Me and Daddy walk away from the fence.

"Let me get on your back and ride," I say.

"Can't you walk sometime," Daddy says. "What you think I'm educating you for—to treat me like a horse?"

V

Mr. George Williams drives his car to the side of the road, then we get out. "Look like we got company," Mr. George Williams says.

Me and Daddy and Mr. George Williams go over where the people is. The people got a little fire burning, and some of them's sitting on the car fender. But most of them's standing round the little fire.

"Welcome," somebody says.

"Thanks," Daddy says. "Since this is my car you sitting on."

"Oh," the man says. He jumps up and the other two men jump up, too. They go over to the little fire and stand round it.

"We didn't mean no harm," one of them say.

Daddy goes over and peeps in the car. Then he opens the door and gets in. I go over to the car where he is.

"Go stand 'side the fire," Daddy says.

"I want get in with you," I say.

"Do what I tell you," Daddy says.

I go back to the fire, and I turn and look at Daddy in the car. Daddy passes his hand all over the car; then he just sit there quiet-like. All the people round the fire look at Daddy in the car. I can hear them talking real low.

After a little while, Daddy opens the door and gets out. He comes over to the fire.

"Well," he says, "I guess that's it. You got a rope?"

"In the trunk," Mr. George Williams says. "What you go'n do, drag it off the highway?"

"We can't burn it out here," Daddy says.

"He say he go'n burn it," somebody at the fire says.

"I'm go'n burn it," Daddy says. "It's mine, ain't it?"

"Easy, Eddie," Mr. George Williams says.

Daddy is mad but he don't say any more. Mr. George Williams looks at Daddy, then he goes over to his car and gets the rope.

"Ought to be strong enough," Mr. George Williams says.

He hands Daddy the rope, then he goes and turns his car around. Everybody at the fire looks at Mr. George Williams backing up his car.

"Good," Daddy says.

Daddy gets between the cars and ties them together. Some of the people come over and watch him.

"Y'all got a side road anywhere round here?" he asks.

"Right over there," the man says. "Leads off back in the field. You ain't go'n burn up that good car for real, is you?"

"Who field this is?" Daddy asks.

"Mr. Roger Medlow," the man says.

"Any colored people got fields round here anywhere?" Daddy asks.

"Old man Ned Johnson 'bout two miles farther down the road," another man says.

"Why don't we just take it on back to the plantation?" Mr. George Williams says. "I doubt if Mr. Claude'll mind if we burnt it there."

"All right," Daddy says. "Might as well."

Me and Daddy get in his car. Some of the people from the fire run up to Mr. George Williams's car. Mr. George Williams tells them something, and I see three of them jumping in. Mr. George Williams taps on the horn, then we get going. I sit 'way back in the seat and look at Daddy. Daddy's quiet. He's sorry because he got to burn up his car.

We go 'way down the road, then we turn and go down the quarter. Soon 's we get down there, I hear two of the men in Mr. George Williams's car calling to the people. I sit up in the seat and look out at them. They standing on the fenders, calling to the people.

"Come on," they saying. "Come on to the car-burning party. Free. Everybody welcome. Free."

We go farther down the quarter, and the two men keep on calling.

"Come on, everybody," one of them says.

"We having a car-burning party tonight," the other one says. "No charges."

The people start coming out on the galleries to see what all the racket is. I look back and I see some out in the yard, and some already out in the road. Mr. George Williams stops in front of Gran'mon's house.

"You go'n tell Amy?" he calls to Daddy. "Maybe she like to go, since you doing it all for her."

"Go tell your mama come on," Daddy says.

I jump out the car and run in the yard.

"Come on, everybody," one of the men says.

"We having a car-burning party tonight," the other one says. "Everybody invited. No charges."

I pull Gran'mon's door open and go in. Mama and Uncle Al and Gran'mon's sitting at the fireplace.

"Mama, Daddy say come on if you want see the burning," I say.

"See what burning?" Gran'mon asks. "Now don't tell me that crazy nigger going through with that."

"Come on, Mama," I say.

Mama and Uncle Al get up from the fireplace and go to the door.

"He sure got it out there," Uncle Al says.

"Come on, Mama," I say. "Come on, Uncle Al."

"Wait till I get my coat," Mama says. "Mama, you going?"

"I ain't missing this for the world," Gran'mon says. "I still think he's bluffing."

Gran'mon gets her coat and Uncle Al gets his coat; then we go on outside. Plenty people standing round Daddy's car now. I can see more people opening doors and coming out on the galleries.

"Get in," Daddy says. "Sorry I can't take but two. Mama, you want ride?"

"No, thanks," Gran'mon says. "You might just get it in your head to run off in that canal with me in there. Let your wife and child ride. I'll walk with the rest of the people."

"Get in, honey," Daddy says. "It's getting cold out there."

Mama takes my arm and helps me in; then she gets in and shuts the door.

"How far down you going?" Uncle Al asks.

"Near the sugar house," Daddy says. He taps on the horn and Mr. George Williams drives away.

"Come on, everybody," one of the men says.

"We having a car-burning party tonight," the other one says. "Everybody invited."

Mr. George Williams drives his car over the railroad tracks. I look back and I see plenty people following Daddy's car. I can't see Uncle Al and Gran'mon, but I know they back there, too.

We keep going. We get almost to the sugar house,

then we turn down another road. The other road is bumpy and I have to bounce on the seat.

"Well, I reckon this's it," Daddy says.

Mama don't say nothing to Daddy.

"You know it ain't too late to change your mind," Daddy says. "All I got to do is stop George and untie the car."

"You brought matches?" Mama asks.

"All right," Daddy says. "All right. Don't start fussing."

We go a little farther and Daddy taps on the horn. Mr. George Williams stops his car. Daddy gets out his car and go and talk with Mr. George Williams. Little bit later I see Daddy coming back.

"Y'all better get out here," he says. "We go'n take it down the field a piece."

Me and Mama get out. I look down the headland and I see Uncle Al and Gran'mon and all the other people coming. Some of them even got flashlights because it's getting dark now. They come where me and Mama's standing. I look down the field and I see the cars going down the row. It's dark, but Mr. George Williams got bright lights on his car. The cars stop and Daddy get out his car and go and untie the rope. Mr. George Williams goes and turns around and come back to the headland where all the people standing. Then he turns his lights on Daddy's car so everybody can see the burning. I see Daddy getting some gas out the tank.

"Give me a hand down here," Daddy calls. But that don't even sound like Daddy's voice.

Plenty people run down the field to help Daddy. They get round the car and start shaking it. I see the car leaning; then it tips over.

"Well," Gran'mon says. "I never would've thought it."

I see Daddy going all round the car with the can, then I see him splashing some inside the car. All the other people back back to give him room. I see Daddy scratching a match and throwing it in the car. He scratches another one and throw that one in the car, too. I see little bit fire, then I see plenty.

"I just do declare," Gran'mon says. " I must be dreaming. He's a man after all."

Gran'mon the only person talking; everybody else is quiet. We stay there a long time and look at the fire. The fire burns down and Daddy and them go and look at the car again. Daddy picks up the can and pours some more gas on the fire. The fire gets big. We look at the fire some more.

"Never thought that was in Eddie," somebody says real low.

"You not the only one," somebody else says.

"He loved that car more than he loved anything."

"No, he must love her more," another person says.

The fire burns down again. Daddy and them go and look at the car. They stay there a good while, then they come out to the headland where we standing.

"What's that, George?" Mama asks.

"The pump," Mr. George Williams says. "Eddie gived it to me for driving him to get his car."

"Hand it here," Mama says.

Mr. George Williams looks at Daddy, but he hands the pump to Mama. Mama goes on down the field with the pump and throws it in the fire. I watch Mama coming back.

"When Eddie gets paid Saturday, he'll pay you," Mama says. "You ready to go home, Eddie?"

Daddy nods his head.

"Sonny," Mama says.

I go where Mama is and Mama takes my hand. Daddy raises his head and looks at the people standing round looking at us.

"Thank y'all," he says.

Me and Mama go in Gran'mon's house and pull the big bundle out on the gallery. Daddy picks the bundle up and puts it on his head, then we go up the quarter to us house. Mama opens the gate and me and Daddy go in. We go inside and Mama lights the lamp.

"You hungry?" Mama asks Daddy.

"How can you ask that?" Daddy says. "I'm starving."

"You want eat now or after you whip me?" Mama says.

"Whip you?" Daddy asks. "What I'm go'n be whipping you for?"

Mama goes back in the kitchen. She don't find what she's looking for, and I hear her going outside.

"Where Mama going, Daddy?"

"Don't ask me," Daddy says. "I don't know no more than you."

Daddy gets some kindling out of the corner and puts it in the fireplace. Then he pours some coal oil on the kindling and lights a match to it. Me and Daddy squat down on the fireplace and watch the fire burning.

I hear the back door shut, then I see Mama coming in the front room. Mama's got a great big old switch.

"Here," she says.

"What's that for?" Daddy says.

"Here. Take it," Mama says.

"I ain't got nothing to beat you for, Amy," Daddy says.

"You whip me," Mama says, "or I turn right round and walk on out that door."

Daddy stands up and looks at Mama.

"You must be crazy," Daddy says. "Stop all that foolishness, Amy, and go cook me some food."

"Get your pot, Sonny," Mama says.

"Shucks," I say. "Now where we going? I'm getting tired walking in all that cold. 'Fore you know it I'm go'n have whooping cough."

"Get your pot and stop answering me back, boy," Mama says.

I go to my bed and pick up the pot again.

"Shucks," I say.

"You ain't leaving here," Daddy says.

"You better stop me," Mama says, going to the bundle.

"All right," Daddy says. "I'll beat you if that's what you want."

Daddy gets the switch off the floor and I start crying.

"Lord, have mercy," Daddy says. "Now what?"

"Whip me," Mama says.

"Amy, whip you for what?" Daddy says. "Amy,

please just go back there and cook me something to eat."

"Come on, Sonny," Mama says. "Let's get out of this house."

"All right," Daddy says. Daddy hits Mama two times on the legs. "That's enough," he says.

"Beat me," Mama says.

I cry some more. "Don't beat my mama," I say. "I don't want you to beat my mama."

"Sonny, please," Daddy says. "What y'all trying to do to me—run me crazy? I burnt up the car—ain't that enough?"

"I'm just go'n tell you one more time," Mama says.

"All right," Daddy says. "I'm go'n beat you if that's what you want."

Daddy starts beating Mama, and I cry some more; but Daddy don't stop beating her.

"Beat me harder," Mama says. "I mean it. I mean it."

"Honey, please," Daddy says.

"You better do it," Mama says. "I mean it."

Daddy keeps on beating Mama, and Mama cries and goes down on her knees.

"Leave my mama alone, you old yellow dog," I

say. "You leave my mama alone." I throw the pot at him but I miss him, and the pot go bouncing 'cross the floor.

Daddy throws the switch away and runs to Mama and picks her up. He takes Mama to the bed and

begs her to stop crying. I get on my own bed and cry in the cover.

I feel somebody shaking me, and I must've been sleeping.

"Wake up," I hear Daddy saying.

I'm tired and I don't feel like getting up. I feel like sleeping some more.

"You want some supper?" Daddy asks.

"Uh-huh."

"Get up then," Daddy says.

I get up. I got all my clothes on and my shoes on.

"It's morning?" I ask.

"No," Daddy says. "Still night. Come on back in the kitchen and eat supper."

I follow Daddy in the kitchen and me and him sit down at the table. Mama brings the food to the table and she sits down, too.

"Bless this food, Father, which we're about to receive, the nurse of our bodies, for Christ sake, amen," Mama says.

I raise my head and look at Mama. I can see where she's been crying. Her face is all swole. I look at Daddy and he's eating. Mama and Daddy don't talk, and I don't say nothing, either. I eat my food. We eating sweet potatoes and bread. I'm having a glass of clabber, too.

"What a day," Daddy says.

Mama don't say nothing. She's just picking over her food.

"Mad?" Daddy says.

"No," Mama says.

"Honey?" Daddy says.

Mama looks at him.

"Why I had to beat you?"

"Because I don't want you to be the laughing-stock of the plantation," Mama says.

"Who go'n laugh at me?" Daddy says.

"Everybody," Mama says. "Mama and all. Now they don't have nothing to laugh about."

"Honey, I don't mind if they laugh at me," Daddy says.

"I do mind," Mama says.

"Did I hurt you?"

"I'm all right," she says.

"You ain't mad no more?" Daddy says.

"No," Mama says. "I'm not mad."

Mama picks up a little bit of food and puts it in her mouth.

"Finish eating your supper, Sonny," she says.

"I got enough," I say.

"Drink your clabber," Mama says.

I drink all my clabber and show Mama the glass.

"Go get your book," Mama says. "It's on the dresser."

I go in the front room to get my book.

"One of us got to go to school with him tomorrow," I hear Mama saying. I see her handing Daddy the note. Daddy waves it back. "Here," she says.

"Honey, you know I don't know how to act in no place like that," Daddy says.

"Time to learn," Mama says. She gives Daddy the note. "What page your lesson on, Sonny?"

I turn to the page, and I lean on Mama's leg and let her carry me over my lesson. Mama holds the book in her hand. She carries me over my lesson two times, then she makes me point to some words and spell some words.

"He knows it," Daddy says.

"I'll take you over it again tomorrow morning," Mama says. "Don't let me forget it now."

"Uh-uh."

"Your daddy'll carry you over it tomorrow night,"

Mama says. "One night me, one night you."

"With no car," Daddy says, "I reckon I'll be round plenty now. You think we'll ever get another one, honey?"

Daddy's picking in his teeth with a broom straw.

"When you learn how to act with one," Mama says. "I ain't got nothing against cars."

"I guess you right, honey," Daddy says. "I was going little too far."

"It's time for bed, Sonny," Mama says. "Go in the front room and say your prayers to your daddy."

Me and Daddy leave Mama back there in the kitchen. I put my book on the dresser and I go to the fireplace where Daddy is. Daddy puts another piece of wood on the fire and plenty sparks shoot up in the chimley. Daddy helps me to take off my clothes. I kneel down and lean against his leg.

"Start off," Daddy says. "I'll catch you if you miss something."

"Lay me down to sleep," I say. "I pray the Lord my soul to keep. If I should die before I wake, I pray the Lord my soul to take. God bless Mama and Daddy. God bless Gran'mon and Uncle Al. God bless the church. God bless Miss Hebert. God bless Bill and Juanita." I hear Daddy gaping. "God bless everybody else. Amen."

I jump up off my knees. Them bricks on the fireplace make my knees hurt.

"Did you tell God to bless Johnny Green and Madame Toussaint?" Daddy says.

"No," I say.

"Get down there and tell Him to bless them, too," Daddy says.

"Old Rollo, too?"

"That's up to you and Him for that," Daddy says. "Get back down there."

I get back on my knees. I don't get on the bricks because they make my knees hurt. I get on the floor and lean against the chair.

"And God bless Mr. Johnny Green and Madame Toussaint," I say.

"All right," Daddy says. "Warm up good."

Daddy goes over to my bed and pulls the cover back.

"Come on," he says. "Jump in."

I run and jump in the bed. Daddy pulls the cover up to my neck.

"Good night, Daddy."

"Good night," Daddy says.

"Good night, Mama."

"Good night, Sonny," Mama says.

I turn on my side and look at Daddy at the fire-place. Mama comes out of the kitchen and goes to the fireplace. Mama warms up good and goes to the bundle.

"Leave it alone," Daddy says. "We'll get up early tomorrow and get it."

"I'm going to bed," Mama says. "You coming now?"

"Uh-hunnnnn," Daddy says.

Mama comes to my bed and tucks the cover under me good. She leans over and kisses me and tucks the cover some more. She goes over to the bundle and gets her nightgown, then she goes in the kitchen and puts it on. She comes back and puts her clothes she took off on a chair 'side the wall. Mama kneels down and says her prayers, then she gets in the bed and covers up. Daddy stands up and takes off his clothes. I see Daddy in his big old long white BVD's. Daddy blows out the lamp, and I hear the spring when Daddy gets in the bed. Daddy never says his prayers.

"Sleepy?" Daddy says.

"Uh-uhnnn," Mama says.

I hear Mama and Daddy talking low, but I don't know what they saying. I go to sleep some, but I open my eyes again. It's some dark in the room. I hear Mama and Daddy talking low. I like Mama and Daddy. I like Uncle Al, but I don't like old Gran'mon too much. Gran'mon's always talking bad about Daddy. I don't like old Mr. Freddie Jackson, either. I like Mr. George Williams though. We went riding 'way up the road with Mr. George Williams. We got Daddy's car and brought it all the way back here. Daddy and them turned the car over and Daddy poured some gas on it and set it on fire. Daddy ain't got no more car now. . . . I know my lesson. I ain't go'n wee-wee on myself no more. Daddy's going to school with me tomorrow. I'm go'n show him I can beat Billy Joe Martin shooting marbles. I can shoot all over Billy Joe Martin. And I can beat him running, too. He thinks he can run fast. I'm go'n show Daddy I can beat him running. . . . I don't know why I had to say, "God bless Madame Toussaint." I don't like her. And I don't like old Rollo, either. Rollo can bark some loud. He made my head hurt with all that loud barking. Madame Toussaint's old house don't smell good. But us house smell good. I hear Mama and Daddy talking low. I get way under the cover. I go to sleep little bit, but I wake up. I hear Mama and Daddy talking. I like to hear Mama and Daddy talking when they talking good. I go to sleep some more. It's some dark under here. It's warm. I feel good way under here.

Author's Note

I was born on a plantation like the one in this book, and I can still remember the people going out into the fields. *A Long Day in November* could have happened in the late 1930s or in the mid 1940s. There was a one-room schoolhouse on or near every plantation, and all classes were taught by one teacher. An older boy or an older girl would assist the teacher with her younger students. One of the bigger boys would build the fire in the heater and see that the schoolhouse stayed warm all day.

But since World War II the land and the schools have changed tremendously. The one-room schoolhouses are no longer there; school buses take the children to a larger school in town. Machinery now has taken over the cane cutting that the people used to do by hand. One cane-cutting machine operated by two or three men can cut as much cane as fifty men could cut by hand. So the people who used to go into the fields with their cane knives have had to seek work elsewhere. Many of them moved to small towns and to the cities looking for whatever kind of work was available. The houses where the people once lived have been torn down, and cane or some other crop has been planted there. About the only people still living on the plantations now are old people who are too tired and too burden-laden to pick up and start all over again. They live on welfare, they raise a few chickens, one or two pigs, and they raise a little garden beside or behind the house. Most of them have electricity and some of them even have gas heaters. Still, there are some who use fireplaces to heat their rooms and use a coal-oil lamp for light.

I want to include a few words about Madame Toussaint and say something about voodooism. In nineteenth-century Louisiana voodooism was as popular in some areas, espe-cially around New Orleans, as is the belief in psychiatry today. Not only did illiterate black people believe in voo-dooism, but many of the educated, rich white people visited the voodoo queen for advice about love, money, politics, or anything else that was troubling them.

To this day voodoo queens are still with us. Of course we are more sophisticated and don't go to them as much as people did a hundred years ago, but they still exist because some people still support them. The Madame Toussaints can be found in almost any large metropolitan area. But they are not called voodoo queens; today they are called healers.

As a final word I would like to say again that life as described in *A Long Day in November* is just about gone. Technology has destroyed it, and I think all for the best. The work on the plantation was hard and tedious. There was not much else to do but go into the fields and work, come home to rest, then go back to work again. Technology—the cane cutter, cotton picker, hay-bailing machines—took this work and forced the people off the land. In the cities the children were able to go to better schools and seek better jobs. Of course the computers are taking over many of these jobs today. So again the people will be forced to work elsewhere. But I have confidence that they will find it.

Ernest J. Gaines
San Francisco, 1971